Stranglehold

At that moment all hell broke loose. Both interlopers started shooting. The stable was filled with gun thunder and spurting muzzle flame. Kelf flowed into action with his customary speed, firing a shot before his gun barely cleared its holster. The nearest man, holding the can, was hit as he squeezed off his first shot. He jerked and buckled at the knees, struck dead centre by Kelf's deadly shooting. Wreathed in gun smoke, his gun spilled from his hand and he sprawled on the ground, jerking spasmodically. Thompson stepped level with Kelf, thrust his shot gun forward and squeezed the trigger. The long gun blasted like a cannon and the second man seemed to fade away, blood spurting from multiple wounds caused by the whirling load of buckshot. He went down like a leaf blowing in a storm.

Stranglehold

Corba Sunman

A Black Horse Western

ROBERT HALE

© Corba Sunman 2017
First published in Great Britain 2017

ISBN 978-0-7198-2216-2

The Crowood Press
The Stable Block
Crowood Lane
Ramsbury
Marlborough
Wiltshire SN8 2HR

www.bhwesterns.com

Robert Hale is an imprint
of The Crowood Press

Typeset by
Derek Doyle & Associates, Shaw Heath
Printed and bound in Great Britain by
CPI Group (UK) Ltd, Croydon, CR0 4YY

ONE

Brent Kelf came out of the hills in west Texas, and the smell of pines faded slowly from his nostrils as he halted his grey horse to peer at the abrupt change of scenery – they had been above the tree-line for three days, and now the vastness of the Texas plain seemed illimitable. But Kelf had eyes only for the little township some three miles ahead that was huddled in the shade of a hill. He leaned his hands on his saddle horn and stretched his back and shoulders against the stiffness of long hours of travel. When he gazed at the town he saw a huge rock seemingly balanced on a high rim, and nodded in satisfaction. Temple Rock, he thought, and was pleased that his brother's instructions for reaching the town had been so accurate.

He dismounted, trailed his reins, and walked a few stiff paces away from the trees. He could see a trail ahead, emerging from the town and running from right to left in a northerly direction. A buckboard was moving along it, coming from the town. He remounted and set out to intercept the wagon, aware that his brother's ranch was in the same direction. His grey quickly hit a lope, and Brent was relieved that the end of his long trip was in sight. He had travelled down from Kansas in response to a letter from John's wife Josie, whom he had never met.

At twenty-seven, Kelf was a big man in a big country. He stood at three inches over six feet, had wide shoulders and a narrow waist. His features were those that most women found attractive – a wide smile, and blue eyes that had set many female hearts fluttering along the trails he had ridden and the towns he had passed through. He could handle any job that was available in the West, although he had very soon decided that punching cows was not his ideal way of earning a living. He had tried the law, and worked as a deputy marshal in Dodge City but left the job after a couple of months to try life as a bounty hunter, which suited him better. His proficiency with weapons made the venture successful.

He was dressed in a grey town suit, wore a white Stetson, and brown leather riding boots. A cartridge belt encircled his waist, glinting with .45 brass shells, and a Colt's Peacemaker pistol was holstered on his right side. He carried a smaller two-shot hand gun in his pocket.

He soon overhauled the wagon, and was just behind it when he heard the sound of hoof beats at his back. He glanced over his shoulder, saw two riders coming up fast, and noted that one of them was drawing a pistol. He frowned as he touched spurs to his grey and went forward quickly to move in beside the buckboard. A young woman was driving the team. She was wearing an eye-catching blue dress and had a small child tied to the seat at her side. She glanced sideways at him when she realized that she was no longer alone, and her expression changed abruptly. She picked up her whip and swung it in his direction. He ducked the blow, but felt a sharp pain in his right shoulder. He reined away as she whipped the team and drew rapidly away from him.

She looked scared, Brent thought, and turned his attention to the two riders flogging their mounts to catch up. They were range dressed, and he assumed they were from a nearby ranch. He slowed his mount to await their arrival, but they swung away from the trail when he turned and rode for the hills to the west. Brent sent the grey on again and rode after the wagon. The woman turned her head to look at him, and when she saw the two riders moving away she slowed her team and brought the buckboard to a halt, applied the brake and picked up a Winchester rifle leaning at her side.

Brent approached carefully, his right hand raised to show his intentions were peaceful.

She covered him with the rifle, and he gained the impression that she was handy with the weapon and was not afraid to use it.

'Hi,' he greeted. 'I hope I didn't scare you, sneaking

up like I did, but those two riders looked like they were intent on accosting you, and one of them was holding his pistol.'

'I caught you with my whip.' She saw a trace of blood on his right shoulder. 'Those two riders are from the AS ranch – the Stratton spread – a couple of no-goods named Fenton and Pardoe. They have a habit of making themselves a nuisance to lone women in town or on the trail.' She paused and looked him over more intently. 'You're a stranger hereabouts. I didn't see you in town earlier.'

'I'm looking for my brother's ranch. He's John Kelf. I'm Brent Kelf. Do you know him?'

'I know him very well.' Her attractive face took on another degree of beauty as she smiled. 'He's the man I married four years ago.' She turned to the toddler at her side and ruffled his fair hair. 'I'm Josie Kelf, and this is our son Billy. Say hello to your Uncle Brent, Billy.'

The boy peered at Kelf from the safety of his mother's skirt, and then buried his face out of sight. Kelf laughed.

'We'll get to know each other pretty quick, Billy,' he said. He turned his head when he heard approaching hoof beats, and a frown appeared on his face when he saw Fenton and Pardoe returning. 'They don't look friendly,' he observed. 'Have they ever given you any trouble?'

'Not in the past. They have stopped the buckboard and looked through my supplies, but I put it down to cowboy fun.'

'It doesn't look funny now. You'd better push on to the ranch. I'll drop back and see what they want, and then I'll follow you.'

She looked into his eyes, shaking her head. 'It would be better if you stayed with me and we kept moving,' she suggested. 'There's a lot of trouble on this range, and you shouldn't get caught up in it.'

'Is that why you wrote asking me to visit?' he countered. 'It'll be all right. You get out of here and I'll come along when I know what those two gents have in mind.'

A shadow crossed her face and she picked up the whip – flicked it across the backs of the horses. When the wagon moved on, Kelf turned to face the riders, his smile disappearing, and a cold expression filtered into his blue eyes.

The two men came up fast, raising dust, and they separated as they closed in. They looked mean, and when the second man pulled his pistol, Kelf knew he was in for it. He reached to his holster and his right hand came up filled with gun metal. The man on the right fired a shot and gun smoke blossomed. The bullet crackled in Kelf's right ear as it narrowly missed him. He cocked his gun and fired instantly, whirling his horse to the left as the shot crashed. He paused just long enough to see his target pitch out of the saddle before looking for the second rider.

A gun crashed and Kelf felt a flash of pain in his left forearm just below the elbow. His pistol lifted into aim, he swung the weapon to allow for the man's movement and then fired a single shot. The man went out of his saddle and the horse ran on free, chasing after the buckboard. Gun echoes grumbled away to the horizon. Kelf swallowed the sharp taste of gun smoke that blew back into his face. He glanced around. The wagon was disappearing over a rise. The two strangers were lying motionless where they had fallen, and Kelf wondered how he had been caught up so suddenly in such a violent situation. He was a stranger to the two men he had shot, but they had been intent on killing him.

He rode to where the nearest man was sprawled in the grass. A gun lay close to the body. The man was dead, a bullet hole in the side of his chest showing where Kelf's bullet had caught him. His eyes were open, already glazing. Kelf turned to the second man, who was likewise dead, and a sigh escaped him as he saw blood running freely into the grass from a bullet-torn throat.

There had been no time for deliberate aiming. They were going to kill him, reason unknown, and he had stopped them in their tracks. For them it was over, but Kelf knew his trouble was just beginning. He rode on along the trail in the direction taken by the buckboard.

Josie had stopped the wagon just over the rise, and when Kelf reached her he saw she was standing up with the rifle in her hands, and he realized she had been covering him.

'I saw what happened,' she said in a flat tone. 'They shot at you and you put them down with single shots. That sure was some shooting, Brent! You must have done a lot of practice to get so fast and accurate. I'm not sure now that I should have written to you.'

'I'm John's brother, and if he is in some kind of trouble then this is where I should be. If the boot was on the other foot he would help me out. So what's the trouble you spoke about, and where do those two men come into it?'

Josie shook her head slowly. 'I think I'll let John tell you. We're not far from the ranch. I just hope John is all right. I hate leaving him alone.'

'He can take care of himself! He's two years older than me, and could always handle himself.'

'Not at the moment. He broke his left leg below the knee a couple of months back and can't get around much yet. He sits in a chair by a window in the house with a rifle in his hands, waiting for trouble to strike.'

'So that's the problem, huh? Let's get moving. The sooner I talk to him the better.'

'What about those two men?'

Kelf's mouth twisted. 'They are dead. They'll wait until I can get around to toting them into town and reporting to the sheriff.'

'And that's when your trouble will start.'

'I'm used to trouble.' He raised his left arm and thrust his hand into the front of his shirt. Blood showed on his sleeve. He saw Josie's face change, and

11

she gasped.

'You've been hurt!'

'It's a scratch. It will keep. Let's get on to the ranch.' He shook his reins and the grey moved forward as Josie set the team in motion. They followed the trail through a stand of trees, and when they emerged, Kelf saw a small ranch house ahead, built of wood. A stream glinted in the sunlight. There were riders moving around in the yard, and blue gun smoke was drifting on the breeze. The sound of shooting carried easily over the distance.

Josie uttered a cry of horror and whipped the team. Kelf uttered a curse and spurred his horse after her. He rode to the team and grasped the rein on the nearer horse, pulling the team to a halt.

'Let go!' Josie cried. 'John is helpless in the house.'

'Stay here out of harm's way and I'll ride on to check,' Kelf snapped. 'Think of Billy, Josie.'

He went on. The grey hit a gallop and he crossed the range, his eyes bleak and his teeth clenched. He noted four men attacking the house, and a rifle inside the building was replying steadily. Kelf drew his pistol and rode into the yard. One of the four attackers had dismounted and was sneaking in to get close to the door of the house. Kelf fired without warning, aiming for a shoulder shot. The man jerked as the chunk of lead tore into him. He fell instantly and remained motionless.

The other three riders swung around to face Kelf,

their guns hammering. He shifted his aim and fired. The nearest horseman flopped out of his saddle, his face pushing into the grass. The remaining two parted, riding in opposite directions across the yard. They continued to shoot at Kelf, and he dropped another instantly. The lone survivor swung his horse and rode for a corner of the house to get out of sight. He was almost out of sight when Kelf squeezed his trigger. The rider swayed drunkenly in his saddle, dropped his gun, and grasped his saddle horn. He was beyond the corner when he fell to the ground.

Gun echoes faded away across the range. Sweat trickled down Kelf's face. He looked around. The trouble had evaporated. He eased nearer to the open doorway of the ranch house and paused.

'Hey, John,' he called. 'This is your brother Brent out here. I think your attackers are finished for the moment.'

He paused for a reply. There was silence for long moments, and then John Kelf replied.

'I recognize your voice, Brent. Come on in. I'm sure glad you've turned up. Josie told me yesterday she wrote you. You're welcome right now.'

Kelf holstered his pistol and stepped into the house. His brother was stretched out on a couch, armed with a Winchester. His left leg was propped up on a stool, splinted and tightly bandaged. He looked pale, but a big grin was showing on his face.

'Hey, I'm glad to see you, Brent. Josie's gone into town for supplies. She took our son with her. I'm expecting her back any time now.'

'I met her on the trail. She's not far away. I'll call her in.' Kelf turned in the doorway and stuck his head outside. He could see the wagon coming in. He reached for his pistol when his gaze alighted on two riders coming across the yard from the right, and relaxed slightly when he spotted the glint of a law badge on the chest of one of them.

'A couple of riders are coming in,' he announced. 'One of them is wearing a law badge.'

'Is he a big man riding a black horse?' John demanded.

'He's big, and he's astride a black horse, if that means anything. How come you're knee deep in trouble, John?'

'Someone wants this place. My herd was run off last week, and now the trigger men are trying to finish me.' Bitterness sounded in John's voice. 'The county sheriff is doing what he can, but he's out of his depth in this. I reckon I'll have to cut my losses and pull out. I've got Josie and Billy to consider.'

'Hello, the house,' a gruff voice called from the porch. 'It's Sheriff Denton out here.'

'A couple of men were on the trail, making for the buckboard when I came upon Josie,' Kelf said. 'They started shooting at me so I killed them.'

'You killed them!' John's expression hardened and his narrowed eyes showed deep shock. He was similar in colouring and build to his brother, but his face was more weathered and lined with care-wrinkles around

14

his eyes. He broke off as hoof beats sounded close to the porch. 'You turned up here just in time to save my hide, Brent, but if you've killed men then you've landed yourself in deep water.'

'A man is entitled to defend his life,' Kelf said sharply. 'They started the shooting.'

'Can I come in?' The sheriff sounded impatient.

'Sure, come on in,' John replied.

The big man who stepped across the threshold was middle-aged, tough-looking, and had dark eyes under black shaggy brows. He wore a law star on his red shirt, his grey pants tucked into riding boots. A gun belt sagged around his thick waist and the butt of a pistol showed on his right thigh. His gun hand did not stray far from the weapon.

'You're a stranger,' he commented, his eyes unblinking as he took in Kelf's appearance.

'He's my brother Brent,' John said, 'on a visit from Kansas.'

Kelf was looking at the man accompanying the sheriff; tall and lean, with a harsh expression on his hard-bitten face. His blue eyes were cold and unblinking, and his gaze never left Kelf's face. The sheriff noted Kelf's manner and smiled.

'This is my deputy, Pete Carter,' Denton said.

The wagon sounded just outside, and Kelf stepped around the sheriff and went out of the door. Josie was untying Billy from the driving seat of the wagon. She paused and looked at Kelf, her face inscrutable, her eyes showing worry.

'Is John OK?' she asked.

Kelf nodded and held out his arms to take the toddler. Josie pushed her son at Kelf and he took him quickly.

'I heard the shooting here when you rode into the yard,' she said, glancing at the dead men stretched out in the yard. 'How come you're so good with a gun?'

'I must be lucky,' he replied. 'It seems to come natural to me.'

'I wish you could talk John into leaving here.' A shadow of fear showed in her eyes. 'They'll kill him if he doesn't pull out.'

Kelf followed her into the house. Josie went to John's side and bent to kiss him.

'I hear you had some trouble on the trail,' John said.

'It was nothing Brent couldn't handle,' Josie replied. 'It was a good thing he showed up when he did. Those two saddle tramps, Fenton and Pardoe, were on the prod, but they made a bad mistake when they picked on Brent.'

'What happened?' Denton demanded.

'They pulled their guns without warning and started shooting at Brent. He put them down with two shots as slick as you please.'

'Are they dead?' the sheriff demanded, looking at Kelf.

'That's the kind of game I play,' Kelf told him. 'They were trying to kill me.'

16

'Go back along the trail and look at the scene of the shooting, Pete,' Denton said.

The tall deputy departed quickly. Moments later they heard him ride out across the yard.

'I saw bodies lying around the yard when I rode in,' Denton continued.

'Several riders turned up just before Brent arrived,' John said. 'They called for me to get out of the house and take my family with me. They said they were going to burn the place, and if we didn't leave we'd be shot.'

'It was a good thing I turned up when I did,' Kelf said.

'So you showed up and shot the men, huh? Are they all dead?'

'I don't know. I haven't had a chance to check them yet.'

'I'll take a look at them.' Denton turned to the door. 'Come with me, Kelf, and explain the way the shooting happened.'

Kelf handed Billy to Josie and accompanied the sheriff out to the yard. He stood on the porch and watched Denton examine the downed riders. The sheriff came back to him, his face expressionless.

'You said there were four. Where's the other one?'

'He got to the corner of the house as I shot him,' Kelf replied.

Denton walked to the corner and peered around it. A gun blasted almost in his face from around the corner. The sheriff reeled backwards and went down

17

heavily on the boards of the porch. Kelf drew his gun as the fourth man he had shot came out of hiding. There was blood on his shirt. He swung his gun to cover Kelf, who snapped off a shot that drew a splotch of blood from the man's shirt front. The man dropped his gun and followed it to the ground.

Kelf went to the sheriff's side and bent over him. Blood was showing on the law man's right shoulder. He was conscious but shocked. Kelf holstered his gun and dropped to his right knee.

'You'll be OK, Sheriff,' he said. He raised his voice. 'Hey, Josie, can you come out here? The sheriff has been shot.'

Josie appeared in the doorway. She came forward quickly and knelt beside the lawman; she opened his shirt and revealed a bullet hole just above the collar bone. She got to her feet and hurried back into the house, turning her head to speak over her shoulder.

'I'll get bandages and water. Then he'll have to get back to town to the doctor.'

Kelf heaved a sigh and reloaded the spent shells in his pistol. He saw movement by the gate to the yard, and tensed at the sight of three riders entering. They came at a run to the house, and were holding pistols in their hands. Kelf cocked his gun. It wasn't over yet. . . .

TWO

Kelf dropped to one knee as the newcomers drew closer. He cocked his pistol and lifted it, and then Josie's voice, fraught with tension, called from the doorway.

'Don't shoot, Brent. It's Andy Murdoch of Bar M coming in with a couple of his crew. He's about the only friend we have around here.'

Kelf relaxed and the trio came up to the porch and reined in. The foremost was a man in his forties. His Stetson was pushed to the back of his head to reveal a mass of black curly hair. He had dark eyes that were bright and alert. His smile of greeting vanished as he looked around and took in the details of what had occurred. His two riders, hands at their waists, watched stolidly – typical cowhands.

'What's been going on, Miz Kelf?' Murdoch demanded. 'We were following the tracks of the herd that was stole from my range last night when Frank there thought he heard shooting over this way, so we came to check you were OK.' He was looking around as he spoke, and stepped down from his saddle when he saw the sheriff stretched out on the porch. 'It's Tom Denton!' he ejaculated. His gaze swivelled to Kelf. 'Did you shoot him?' he demanded.

'Why should you think I shot him?' Kelf asked.

'You're a stranger here. I've never seen you before.' Murdoch looked over the sheriff and turned to Josie, standing motionless in the doorway. 'He needs the doctor,' he observed.

'I was about to bandage him and then take him into town,' Josie replied. 'Let me introduce you to my brother-in-law Brent Kelf. He's just arrived on a visit from Kansas. Brent, this is Andy Murdoch of Bar M, our neighbour, and the two men with him are Frank Rudd on the left and Sam Faylen.'

'Glad to know you, Brent,' said Murdoch, a smile breaking out briefly on his taut lips.

'It's good to meet someone who doesn't start shooting at me,' Kelf replied. 'What's going on around here?'

'I wish I could answer that question.' Murdoch shook his head. 'I knew John was getting some trouble. And I lost a herd last night – my crew is out looking for tracks left by the rustlers. But you're knee deep in dead men. What happened here?'

Josie went into the house. Kelf explained the events that had occurred since his arrival, and Murdoch whistled through his teeth.

'Perhaps you'll take a look at the hard cases I shot,'

Kelf suggested. 'You might know some of them.' Hoof beats sounded on the hard pan of the yard and they swung around to look at the newcomer riding into the yard. It was the deputy Pete Carter.

'He was here with the sheriff and rode out to check on the two men I shot on the trail,' Kelf said.

Murdoch was frowning when he looked into Kelf's hard gaze. 'There are two more of them on the trail, huh? With you around we'll soon get to the bottom of this little shindig. Frank, you and Sam take a look at the dead men and see if you can recognize any of them. I'll have a talk with Carter. Seeing him here will save us a ride into town.'

Josie emerged from the house carrying a bowl of water and holding a cloth under one arm. Kelf stood beside her while she attended to the unconscious sheriff. When she had finished, she got to her feet, relief showing on her pale face but her eyes revealed that she was badly shocked by what had occurred.

'He'll be OK,' she said. 'His life is not in danger, and Doc Farrell will soon patch him up. Come and have a talk with John. I can't persuade him to leave here and stay in town for a spell. But there's nothing here to hold him. The cattle have been stolen. There's nothing left. He says I can take Billy and stay in town, but he's not going to leave.'

'He'll die here if he stays,' Kelf said starkly. 'I'll talk to him. He'll listen to me.'

They went into the house. John was on his couch, keeping Billy amused. He looked up at his brother, his face harshly set.

'What am I gonna do, Brent?' he demanded. 'I can't leave this place unattended. These hard cases, whoever they are, will burn it to the ground. I want Josie to take Billy into town, but she says she won't go if I stay.'

'So what's the problem? The sheriff will be going to town in the buckboard presently, and you and your family can travel in it. I'm here now, and anyone trying to fire this place will soon find they're on the losing side.'

'It's not your fight,' John said.

'It is,' Kelf retorted sharply. 'I didn't start the shooting this morning, so I am entitled to fight back.'

John relented. His expression changed and he sighed heavily. When he met Kelf's hard gaze, he nodded.

'I guess you're right,' he said, shaking his head. 'I'm useless with this broken leg. But don't take any risks out here, Brent. When I get on my feet again we'll go after the hard cases together.'

The deputy came into the house, followed by Andy Murdoch. 'I checked those two men on the trail,' Carter said, 'and I know them – Fenton and Pardoe. They work for Abel Stratton who owns the AS ranch. Those two are pests around town, getting drunk and making a nuisance around the womenfolk. I don't know how they fit into this but I'm surprised they took to gun play, and just when there's a flare-up of rustling.'

'What kind of a man is Stratton?' Kelf asked.

'He runs the biggest spread in the county, and his crew is tough – real tough.' Carter grimaced. 'They don't tolerate nesters, or even a man riding through. If you'll see to the sheriff getting back to town then I'll mosey along to AS and have a jaw with Stratton. But I can't believe he's mixed up in this trouble.'

'I'm gonna look around for tracks of the rustled stock taken from here,' Kelf said. 'I reckon it's the best way of getting at the root of the trouble.'

'Don't go out there alone, Brent,' John said harshly. 'I'd never forgive myself if anything happened to you.'

'What brand do you use?' Kelf countered.

'The Big K. The rustlers took nearly one thousand head, and I couldn't leave the house to look for them,' John added bitterly.

'I'll do it for you.' Kelf drew his pistol and checked it. 'I'll come into town to see you if I do learn anything.' He moved to the door, clearly impatient to get moving.

'I'll ride with you,' Carter said. 'It's on my way to Stratton's spread.'

'I'm gonna look for the thieves who took my herd last night,' Murdoch said. 'Frank, stick around here until this family is ready to pull out and then escort them into town and see that they're safe before you come back to me.'

Josie followed Kelf out to the porch. She looked troubled.

'I really started something when I wrote to you,' she said hesitantly.

'It was the best thing you could have done,' he replied. 'Where will you stay in town?'

'My father is Jeff Thompson. He owns the freight line; has a big house on Main Street in Temple Rock. His freight depot is on the back lot behind the house. We'll stay with him. He's got some tough men working for him who will stand up for us if we get any more trouble.'

'That's good to know.' Kelf swung into his saddle. 'Where was the herd when it was stolen?' he asked.

'Wait until I've put some provisions in a sack for you,' Josie said.

'I've got some stuff, but it won't hurt to take some more.' He curbed his impatience, not liking the thought of the cattle thieves getting clear.

Pete Carter emerged from the house. His deputy badge glinted on his chest.

'I'm ready to ride when you are,' he said. 'John has told me where his herd was taken from. With a bit of luck, we could come up with the rustlers at the river crossing by Moore's trading post.'

Josie came out of the house with a gunny sack filled with provisions. Kelf dismounted and fixed the sack to his cantle.

'Take care,' Josie said.

'I'll be back,' he replied. 'It shouldn't take us long to deal with the rustlers.'

Carter laughed bleakly. 'I wish I had your optimism,'

he observed.

They rode out, circled the house, and Carter led the way across the deserted range. Within an hour, they were looking at cattle tracks – a large herd that trailed away to the north-east. Kelf dismounted and looked around for horse tracks. He found plenty. Seven men had pushed his brother's steers off their home range. Kelf studied the tracks – their only link with the rustlers – and made a sketch on the back of an envelope of several that were abnormal. One had lost a nail and part of the shoe. Another shoe had twisted on a rock and was bent forward out of alignment.

'How do you think that will help you?' Carter demanded.

'If I can find the horse that left the print then I'm certain to find its rider. It'll be proof, won't it, and that's something you lawmen are always talking about.'

'We'll know the rustlers when we catch up with them,' Carter said. 'They'll be with the herd, and that will be good enough for me.'

They continued, and made good time with the tracks plain to follow. The hours passed seemingly slowly under the hot sun and, as evening neared, Carter began to look around for a campsite for the night.

'How far is it to that trading post you mentioned?' Kelf asked.

'That's Elroy Moore's place.' Carter nodded. 'It's

about ten miles from here.'

'Wouldn't it be better to ride in there now and have a look? We might catch the rustlers off guard. And Moore would have some good information if he saw the herd pass his place.'

'You're right.' Carter spoke without hesitation. 'I should have thought of that. Come on. Let's forget about tracks for now. We can always come back here to pick up signs if Moore can't help us.'

They rode on at a steady lope, and reached the trading post just as the sun was going down. Shadows had already filled the low places on the range and stars were brightening in the darkening sky. Kelf saw the river off to the left, glinting in the last of the sunlight. The trading post was one storey, made of adobe, sprawling along the river bank, looking derelict without lights showing. As they drew nearer, a couple of low windows became dimly illuminated, and Kelf noted a big corral off to one side which contained at least a dozen horses.

'Moore has got customers,' Carter observed. 'He gets a lot of business from neighbouring farms and ranches. Let's move in quiet like, and see what we can find before they can ready for us. Best thing is for you to stay quiet and watch points. I'll talk to Moore. He's usually on the side of the law, but this rustling is the biggest thing to hit the county in a long time, and he just might be getting a cut from the proceeds.'

'I reckon we should check the horses in the corral first,' Kelf suggested. 'If we strike lucky with the hoof prints I sketched then we'll know for a certainty that some of the rustlers are here.'

'That's a real good idea,' Carter agreed. 'There's enough light to inspect the hoofs.'

They rode to the corral and dismounted. Kelf uncoiled the rope hanging from his saddle horn and slipped between the bars of the corral. The dozen horses ran to the other end of the corral. Kelf shook out his rope and went forward slowly, accompanied by Carter.

'Let me rope 'em and you can check the hoofs,' Carter said. 'You know more about that sort of thing than I do.'

Kelf handed his rope to the deputy and they continued. Carter swung the lariat, and the noose settled neatly over the head of a bay. The animal stood still with the rope around its neck. Kelf went forward and checked the animal's hoofs. He removed the noose from the bay and it ran back to the other horses. Carter prepared to lasso another horse.

It was almost full dark by the time they worked through the horses, and there were only four animals to be checked when Carter put the rope on a buckskin and pulled it clear of the other animals. Kelf checked its feet.

'Here's one with a twisted shoe,' Kelf said quickly, 'just like the one I sketched.'

'The hell you say!' Carter laughed. 'Forget about the remaining nags. Let's go talk to the man who owns this buckskin.'

They tied their horses at a hitch rail outside the front door of the trading post and Carter led the way into the dimly lit interior. Kelf looked around quickly. A long bar occupied the back wall facing the door. Merchandise and supplies littered the rest of the floor space in semi-orderly piles, and two big racks on another wall contained a good selection of long guns. A smaller counter to the right of the door contained glass cabinets filled with smaller items for sale.

A huge man was standing behind the bar, a whiskey glass in his right hand, and he was chatting to two range clad men who looked like ranch hands.

'The big man behind the bar is Leroy Moore,' Carter said in an undertone to Kelf as he led the way to the bar. 'I wouldn't trust him out of my sight, but he's been useful in the past. You keep an eye on the five men at that little table to the left and I'll do the talking.'

Kelf had noted the table and its occupants, who were drinking and playing cards. They were range dressed – looked like working cow hands, not drifters. They were watching Carter intently, probably because of the law star on his chest. Carter halted at the bar and leaned his left elbow on it. Kelf looked at Moore, who was wearing a stained apron over his normal clothes. He was overly large in body and limbs. His head was completely bald and lamplight shone on his scalp. He didn't seem particularly clean, and looked as if he slept regularly in his apron. He wore a cartridge belt around his thick waist, which sagged to the holster on his right hip that contained a well-cared for .44 Navy Colt.

'Howdy, Carter,' Moore said in a gravelly voice which seemed to come from his boots. 'What are you doing out this way? You're a long way from home. Is the sheriff with you? I need to talk to him.'

'I can take a message to him when I go back to town. Denton is too busy to ride out at this time.' He snickered. 'Don't tell me he owes you money!'

Kelf smiled, but nobody else did. His gaze slid around the interior of the long room, his sense of smell identifying a number of scents and aromas arising from the merchandise, leather, coffee beans, new clothes and some items that were unidentifiable. The five men at the table continued to play cards, but they seemed to have more interest in what was going on at the bar, and the two men drinking at the bar were frozen in their positions, merely raising their glasses to their lips and gulping down their poor whiskey while their eyes watched all and sundry.

'So what's going on in your part of the range?' Moore asked in his rasping tone. He was the only one of those present who seemed to be unbothered by Carter's presence.

'The usual thing,' Carter replied. 'In town bad men are still trying to make a quick buck; rustlers are stealing the range blind and dead men are lying around all over the place.'

'I ain't heard anything about that kind of trouble!'

29

Moore rasped. 'Is that happening in town?'

Carter glanced at Kelf, saw that he was watching the five card players with his right hand relaxed at his side. When Carter spoke there was an edge to his tone, and his words cracked through the silence.

'Which of you owns the buckskin out in the corral?' he demanded abruptly.

One of the two cow hands standing at the bar turned to face Carter, his hand dropping to the butt of his holstered pistol. He was a diminutive man, slightly built, but his brown eyes were mean. Aggression seeped out of his squat body.

'The buckskin is mine,' he rasped. 'What's it to you, Deputy?'

'I was checking for rustler tracks earlier and your buckskin's prints were among those I found. I trailed them right into the corral outside. Get your hand away from your waist and stand still. I'm arresting you on suspicion of rustling.'

'The hell you are! Where did you see those hoof prints, and how do you know my buckskin made 'em?'

'They were on the Big K ranch that was robbed of one thousand head last night.'

'Well, you'd better start looking someplace else for the rustlers. I work for Abel Stratton – have done for three years, and I was in the bunk house on the ranch last night when you say I was out rustling.' He turned to his tall companion. 'Ain't that so, Hank?'

'Sure it is, and there were about ten others who

can back you up, Shorty.'

'We'll go into that stuff later,' Carter said. 'I'll put you in jail and hold your horse as evidence. I've got witnesses who will say that buckskin was with the rustlers last night. What's your name, Shorty?'

Shorty's face was mottled with anger, and his hand edged towards his holstered gun.

'I'm Joe Kett, and no one can get away with calling me a rustler,' he said in a rising tone. 'You got a nerve, Deputy, coming in here and accusing a man of being a rustler.'

'I ain't accused you. All you got to do is prove you weren't with your horse when it was with the horses the rustlers used. Just raise your hands and don't make a play for your gun or I'll be forced to shoot you. And if I don't get you then the man with me will surely put you down. He's killed six men already today so he's had plenty of practice.'

Shorty was shocked by the words, and gazed at Kelf with an unblinking gaze while he considered what he had heard.

'You killed six men today?' he demanded.

'They ain't been buried yet so you can count them for yourself if you don't believe the deputy,' Kelf said. 'Now, talk about your buckskin. Were you in the saddle last night when he helped the other horses to steal my brother's herd?'

Shorty drew a deep breath, restrained it for some moments while the silence deepened inside the trading post, and then exhaled sharply and drew his pistol. The quick movement took everyone present by surprise, with the exception of Kelf, who reacted like lightning when he caught Shorty's initial movement. His pistol appeared in his hand, and blasted before Shorty could complete his action.

The crash of the gun sent shock waves across the dimly illuminated room and rattled bottles on the back shelf. Shorty jumped spasmodically as the bullet broke his right forearm. His gun spun out of his hand and fell at Carter's feet. Carter bent and picked it up. Shorty fell against his taller companion and then slipped to the floor, yelping in agony. The gun echoes faded quickly. Carter stared at Shorty, grimaced, and said to Kelf, 'You didn't kill him!'

'I reckoned you'd want to question him,' Kelf replied.

'That's a good idea.' Carter grinned. He gazed at the writhing Shorty for a moment, and then added, 'You ain't dead, Shorty, so get on your feet and start telling the truth. We've got evidence against you, and unless you can make me believe otherwise then you're heading straight to jail in Temple Rock.'

Kelf retained his gun in his hand and faced the five men seated around the card table. The clicks as he cocked his pistol sounded menacing. He covered the table, the muzzle of his gun seeming to inspect each of the motionless men in turn, like a hound dog scenting a possum.

'You in the black Stetson with the silver hat band,' Kelf said. 'You're nursing your gun under the table, and if you don't drop it now I'll put a bullet in your belly where you can't digest it.'

The gun thumped on the hard earthen floor and Carter went across to the table and collected it.

'I know you by sight,' he said to the man. 'You ride for Stratton. What are you doing in here in the middle of the week? Stratton doesn't allow his crew to leave the ranch except at weekends. You've got some talking to do, mister, and you better tell the truth.'

A gun exploded into smoke and flame, and the lamp on the bar disintegrated. Kelf dived to the floor as the big room was plunged into darkness, aware that Carter moved at the same time, and they were both flat as several guns came into play and laced the darkness with muzzle flame.

THREE

Kelf did not reply to the shooting. He kept his head down while fiery muzzle flashes split the darkness. He reached out his left hand and made contact with Carter, almost beside him, and tugged at his shoulder. When he started inching full length in the direction of the door, Carter followed closely. The shooting soon died down until even the occasional shot faded out. Moore's voice suddenly cut through the darkness.

'Hey, cut out the shooting. It's my merchandise that's getting damaged, and trade ain't so good these days. Put up your guns and I'll light another lamp. You can talk over the deputy's accusations. He's only jumping to conclusions, so put him straight on who you are and what you do around here. I know all of you by sight, and I'll back you up. So whaddya say? No more shooting and I'll light a lamp.'

There was no answer, and the only sound that came out of the darkness was an occasional groan of pain from Joe Kett.

'Light the goddamn lamp, if you're going to,' Carter said suddenly. 'This darkness ain't good for my nerves. I ain't about to resume shooting. I'm only asking questions, so let's keep this friendly, huh? My gun is in its holster, and it'll stay there unless some jackass starts something.'

Kelf eased to his left until he felt a wall beside him. He could hear Carter's breathing, and was prepared to follow the lawman's lead if Moore did light a lamp. A match scraped and a tiny flame over by the bar moved slightly as Moore tried to locate a lamp. There was no sound in the trading post, and no shooting. The glow increased suddenly as the match touched a lamp wick. Kelf turned his head to study the big room, and was surprised when he saw the small table was deserted. The five men had vanished. Moore was hunched over the lamp, and the room brightened as he adjusted the wick. Joe Kett was crouched on the floor with his taller companion beside him.

'Where the hell did those five men go?' Moore demanded.

'Out through the window behind the table,' Carter observed, getting to his feet. His gun was in his hand, and he covered the fallen Kett as he went back to the bar. 'You're making a big fuss about a bullet in your arm, Kett. Get up and answer some questions.'

'He's hurt bad,' the man beside Kett declared.

'The bullet went through his arm and turned into his stomach.'

'He should've done what he was told,' Carter retorted. 'I reckon you can put names to the five men who were at the table, huh, Moore?'

'What do you want with them?' the trader demanded. 'Do you suspect them of being rustlers?'

'I'd suspect my mother if she could ride a horse,' Carter replied. He went to Joe Kett's side, dropped to one knee and examined him.

'Hell!' he said. 'The bullet finished up in his guts right enough. I'll take him to town and get the doc to take a look at him. What's your name?' he asked the tall cowboy.

'Hank Webber,' the man replied.

'You'll go with me, Webber, and you'll be real lucky if you don't see the inside of my jail. Moore, you've got a wagon, huh? I'll borrow it to take Kett into town.'

'I'll move out, make camp on the trail,' Kelf said, 'and I'll make an early start in the morning to run down the rustled steers. I'll come to town and tell you about it if I have any luck.'

'Be careful out here,' Carter warned. 'A man can disappear without trace and never be found.'

Kelf left the trading post with a sigh of relief. He swung into the saddle of his horse and rode back the way they had come until he reached the spot where they had left the horse tracks. He dismounted, and stood for a long time at the head of his horse, listening to the noises of the night. Star shine was bright. The sky was almost cloudless, and a thin crescent of the moon showed far to the east. When he was satisfied that there was nothing unnatural around him, he unsaddled his horse and made camp.

He ate cold food and drank water, not wanting to risk a camp fire. He knee hobbled his horse, gave it a drink of water out of his Stetson, and then threw down his blanket roll. He settled down, placed his Winchester by his right side, and slid his pistol under the end of his gunny sack of supplies, which he was using as a pillow. Within moments of closing his eyes he was asleep, and knew nothing more until the sun coming above the horizon next morning shone into his eyes and awakened him.

He broke camp quickly, eager now to follow tracks. The trail was broad and fairly fresh, and he rode at a canter, half his attention on the track and the other half watching his surroundings. He expected the rustlers to have someone watching their rear, and his first intimation of having been discovered would be a rifle bullet from cover. He rode for three hours, the tracks always leading into the north east. The range was illimitable, and empty. There was no sign of human life.

The sun wanted about an hour to reach its zenith when a rifle shot shattered the brooding silence of the range. Kelf glanced around quickly, and when he spotted three riders on his left, coming off a skyline and riding to intercept him, he reined in to await their arrival.

Two of the men were holding rifles across their saddles. They were unsmiling, and Kelf noted that they stayed behind the leading man, who arrived with a slithering halt that had his sorrel stopping with its nose across the neck of Kelf's horse. The animal tried to bite Kelf's mount but the black shied away. The sorrel's head came around to Kelf, and it tried to sink its teeth into his left thigh. Kelf drew his pistol, holding his horse under control with his left hand. The stranger spurred his sorrel and the beast reared, hoofs flailing the air as it tried to trample Kelf's black.

'Back off,' Kelf called, 'or I'll put a slug through your skull.'

'You're on AS range,' the man replied. He was big and powerful, over six feet, and wore expensive range clothes. He had a Nordic look about him – yellow hair and keen blue eyes. His expression was hard, his mouth pulled into a slit that was twisted by a bad temper. 'I'm Willard Stratton,' he said in a snarling tone. 'My father is Abel Stratton, and he owns every acre between here and Bent's Crossing. He also owns half the town of Temple Rock, and most of the folk who live in it. You've got a nerve, bracing me on Stratton grass with a gun in your hand.'

'And I'll use it if I have to, so back down and sheath your claws, Stratton. I'm looking for rustlers. They stole a thousand head of cattle from my brother's ranch last night.'

'Who is your brother?'

'John Kelf.'

'And you reckon to find stolen stock on our range?'

'They headed in this direction.' Kelf pointed to the tracks he was following. 'Look for yourself. How come you missed them?'

'Rustlers don't steal steers from AS. If rustlers are moving across our range we'll get onto them. You're lucky, Kelf. Men who ride across this range without permission get a bad time if we catch them.' He grinned, ignoring the menace of Kelf's steady gun, although his eyes had a wary look in them.

'I'm holding my gun, and I wouldn't advise you to try anything or you'll catch a bad dose of lead poisoning. Warn your two men to drop their rifles.'

'If you've got any sense at all, you'll get off our grass as fast as you can, and you'll keep going until you hit the next county.'

Willard Stratton let his hand edge towards the butt of his holstered gun. 'Burke, keep him covered with your rifle. Johnson, shake out your loop and pitch it over this bozo's head. We'll cure him of his sass and knock some sense into him.'

When Kelf saw Burke lift his rifle to his shoulder he set his hand into motion. His pistol lifted and blasted instantly. Willard Stratton ducked wildly as the bullet passed him closely, and his eyes widened when he saw Burke drop his rifle and then sprawl out of his saddle. Johnson was reaching for his lariat but when Burke fell, he sat motionless on his horse, watching Kelf with respect. Stratton set his hand in motion and put his fingers around his pistol. Kelf put a slug through the brim of Stratton's Stetson. Stratton dragged his gun from its holster but released it instantly and it fell to the ground.

'It seems to me you're the one who needs sense knocked into him,' Kelf observed impassively, 'and I'd take on the chore if I didn't have something more important to do. Get rid of any other weapons you might have and then ride back to the skyline you crossed. I don't want to see hide nor hair of you again, Stratton.'

Fury showed in every line of Stratton's face as he lifted his rifle from its saddle boot and dropped it to the ground. He backed his sorrel off and turned away. He and Johnson paused to push the semiconscious Burke across his saddle, and then rode off in the direction from which they came. Kelf sat watching them, and stiffened when, just before they reached the skyline, three riders appeared above them. Willard reined in as altercation passed between him and one of the newcomers. After a few moments all the riders came down the slope to where Kelf was waiting.

The leading rider was one of the newcomers, and Kelf didn't have to wonder who he was. Willard was obviously his son – they were so alike, although the older man was of a different calibre. He reined up in front of Kelf, ignoring the gun in Kelf's hand, and halted with the head of his white horse almost resting on Kelf's thigh. Willard and his men remained in the background. The other two men, who looked like gun slammers, sat their mounts one either side of their boss, their hands close to holstered guns, eyes narrowed, ready to draw their weapons at the drop of a hat.

'I'm Abel Stratton. I own the AS ranch. Put your gun away and tell me why you're trespassing on my range.' Hard blue eyes stared at Kelf, who realized that here was a man who would never back down in any circumstance.

'I explained to your son the reason why I'm here,' Kelf said in a steady tone. 'I guess he told you that when you met him on the rise. These are the tracks of the rustled cattle I'm following.' He pointed to the area of heavily marked ground that showed where a large number of steers had passed. 'I'm gonna follow them clear to Hell and back if I have to. Any honest rancher worth his salt would help a man to run down the thieves, if only to protect his own stock, but all I got from your son were threats if I didn't leave the trail. And that's the reason why my gun will stay in my hand until I'm satisfied you don't intend to run me off your grass.'

'You have my permission to follow these tracks,' Abel Stratton said without hesitation. 'You won't have any trouble from my outfit. I'll send a man with you to ensure that none of my crew will interfere with you.'

41

He whirled his horse about before Kelf could thank him, and rode back up the slope, followed by his two gun slicks. Willard sat his horse watching his father's progress, his face set in harsh lines. He turned back to Kelf.

'We'll be watching you closely,' he grated. 'Don't expect anything from us but hot lead. My old man is getting soft in the head.'

'Thanks for the warning,' Kelf said. 'If you're on the prod for trouble then pick your gun out of the grass and start working it. If there's gonna be a fight between us I'd rather face it now instead of having it creep up on me when I least expect it.'

'Are you calling me a back-shooter?' Willard snarled.

'If the cap fits, wear it,' Kelf replied.

He sat his saddle, motionless and wary, until Willard led his men away in the direction his father had taken. When they disappeared over the skyline, he continued following the tracks of the rustled cattle. . . .

Later, two riders, a man and a woman, appeared on a crest before Kelf and he reined in and drew his pistol. The pair came down a decline at an angle to intercept him. Both were wearing gun belts and pistols, but made no hostile move. The woman was young, dressed in good clothes, half boots, and a flat-crowned Stetson that enhanced her appearance. The man was older, had a seamed, weather-beaten face, tired blue eyes, and wore stained range clothes. He had a pistol holstered on his right hip, and his right hand did not stray far from its butt.

'I saw you take on Willard,' the woman called as she drew near, 'and I didn't believe it when he gave way and rode off. And you shot Burke. I've wanted to do that for a long time.'

Kelf eyed the gun belt around her trim waist and frowned. She was riding a palomino; had a Cheyenne saddle, he could tell, and she looked as if she belonged in a big city instead of on a dusty range in Texas. Her horse was restive, and when it moved around he was surprised to see it was branded AS.

'You're a Stratton,' he said, noting the resemblance between her and Willard Stratton.

'I'm Adelaide Stratton.' She grimaced. 'Willard is my brother, unfortunately.' Her lips twisted as she spoke. 'But worse – Abel Stratton is my father. I'm a prisoner on this spread. I came home from Carson City three months ago, and my father won't let me leave again. Bill Kirk.' She indicated the dour-faced man sitting his horse beside her. 'He's my jailer. He's closer to me than the tail of my horse.'

'It's my job,' Kirk said harshly. 'It's nothing personal. If I didn't do it there would be someone else riding behind you.'

'And who are you?' Adelaide demanded, her eyes quick and bright as a bird's.

'I'm Brent Kelf. My brother owns the Big K ranch. I'm tracking down the rustlers who stole his cattle a couple of nights ago.'

'And they came across AS range?' She shook her head in disbelief and instinctively looked down at the ground. She saw the trail he was obviously following and checked its general direction. When she looked into Kelf's eyes again she seemed more animated. 'It looks like your stock is heading for Rainbow Valley,' she mused. 'Would you like me to show you the way? You'd never find it by yourself. Willard and I found it by accident many years ago, in the days when he was normal and we were friendly.'

'It sounds interesting,' Kelf said. 'How far is it, and why can't I find it for myself? I've only got to follow the tracks.'

'If I show you the place then I would expect you to help me,' she replied.

'To get off this range, I guess,' he said. 'That would bring a whole lot of trouble down on my neck. Why won't your father let you go back to Carson City?'

'I was almost kidnapped soon after I came home, and my father won't run the risk of that happening again.'

'And what will your jailer think of you going along with me?'

'My orders are that she doesn't leave the AS range, and Rainbow Valley is in the high ground to the north,' Kirk said. 'As far as I know, it's OK for her to ride where she likes so long as she stays on Stratton grass.'

'And if I find the rustled cattle in the valley, it will kind of throw suspicion on your father or your brother that they're guilty of rustling, or are you hinting that your family is responsible for it?'

'Help me get away from here and I'll tell you what you want to know.' She dropped her hand to the butt of her .38, drew it and levelled it at Kirk. 'Get rid of your gun, Bill,' she said.

'Now lookee here, Adelaide, this ain't the time to be joshing,' Kirk said slowly. 'Kelf looks like a man who calls a spade a spade and he won't believe you're playing a game. He's likely to shoot me, and all for nothing. You're always too eager to play the fool when you think it will help you, and sometimes your tricks don't go down well with strangers.'

'I ain't likely to shoot anyone who doesn't shoot at me,' Kelf said. 'I'm sorry if you're in some kind of trouble, Miss Stratton, but I need to push on. I have to get to Temple Rock as soon as I can. My brother and his family are heading there right now, and I want to be around to make sure they don't get more trouble. There was some shooting at their place earlier, and I am anxious for their safety.'

'Who was doing the shooting?' Adelaide demanded.

'They were all strangers to me.' Kelf shook his head. 'But I heard the sheriff say two of the men were from your father's crew.'

'That sounds bad.' She shook her head and set her teeth into her prominent lower lip. 'So now it starts. I thought it was only big talk from Willard, but it sounds as if the trouble is starting like he said it

45

would. I've got to get away from here. Please help me, Mr Kelf. I'll make it worth your while if you can get me safely to Temple Rock.'

He watched her face while his mind slipped over the possibilities. 'You'll show me the way into Rainbow Valley before we go to town?' he asked.

'Anything you say.'

'And what do you say about that, Kirk?'

'I've told you what my job is. I'll have to draw on you, mister, if you try to take her off this range.'

Adelaide squeezed the trigger of her pistol and Kirk uttered a cry and slumped in his saddle. Blood showed on his right shoulder. Kelf leaned sideways in his saddle and snatched the gun from her hand. He stepped down from his saddle, went to Kirk's side, and was relieved to see that the old man was not badly hurt. The .38 slug had creased his shoulder. Kelf helped him out of leather and turned to Adelaide, who sat her mount with a half smile on her lips.

'Get off your horse and see what you can do for him,' Kelf said sharply. 'You didn't have to shoot him!'

'You can see how desperate I am,' she said. 'He'll be all right. He can make it back to the ranch house. By the time they can send someone out to look for us we'll be long gone.'

Kelf rummaged in his saddle bag and found a white cloth he kept for emergencies. He bared the flesh wound on the top of Kirk's right shoulder,

46

washed away the blood, and bound the cloth around the shoulder. When he had finished he boosted Kirk back in his saddle and handed him the reins.

'Go on back to the ranch,' he said, and slapped the horse on the rump. Kirk groaned as the horse went forward, but he maintained his seat and headed for the nearest rise.

Adelaide accompanied Kelf in silence, and they changed direction and headed for the high ground to the north, following the cattle tracks leading in the same direction.

By late afternoon they were in broken ground and ascending an incline. The range had given way to sand and rock – bad land that could not support cattle.

'How much farther to Rainbow Valley?' asked Kelf when they paused to give their mounts a breather.

'See that highest point up there to our right? When we reach there you'll be able to look down into Rainbow Valley from the rim rock. The entrance is over to the left a couple miles, and the rustlers will have blotted the cattle tracks in all directions. But there is a couple of game trails going down into the valley from this side and you could come back here after you've taken me to Temple Rock and get down there among the rustlers. There are only half a dozen men left with the stolen cows.'

Kelf looked around. 'Let's push on,' he said. 'I need to see the rustled stock in the valley before I'll be satisfied. Then we'll head for Temple Rock.

Judging by the twists and turns we've made coming here, we can ride at an angle and cut down the distance we have to travel.'

'You evidently know this range well,' she observed.

'I arrived at my brother's ranch yesterday morning for the first time. I'm a stranger here. What will you do when you get to town? Do you have friends there? I reckon your father will have search parties out looking for you before you can get clear.'

'I'll be OK,' she told him. 'I'll get by.'

When they reached a stretch of ground which angled upward more sharply, Adelaide reined in and dismounted. She sat down on a nearby rock and smiled at Kelf.

'This is as far as I go. I'll wait for you to get back. Go up to the highest point and the layout of the valley will be quite plain to you. Be careful, because those rustlers are alert all the time, and if you get spotted they'll come out after you like a swarm of bees.'

Kelf took his Winchester and went on. He was breathing hard when he got to the top of the incline, and when he paused to look around he was amazed by the sight awaiting his gaze. Rainbow Valley stretched from north to south in a series of gentle slopes covered with lush grass, and he spotted grazing cattle. He crouched in cover, mindful of Adelaide's warning, and although he searched the valley carefully he did not see any sign of human habitation. There was a scattering of trees over on the far side, and the glint of a stream caught his eye. It wended its way down from higher ground farther north, and opened out into a fair-sized creek just over halfway along the valley.

Satisfied, he eased back out of sight of the valley and took precautions as he returned the way he had come. The heavy silence which overlaid the wilderness pressed down like an extra blanket on a hot night. When he reached his horse, standing with trailing reins exactly where he had left it, he halted with a jolt, for Adelaide and her horse were gone. . . .

FOUR

Kelf checked his surroundings, looking for movement among the rocks, but nothing stirred. There was not even a sign of dust in the air. He studied the ground, looking for hoof prints, but the whole area was solid rock. For once in his life he was uncertain about what he should do next. But his priorities sorted themselves out in his mind and he decided to start his search from the entrance to Rainbow Valley. He thought it was unlikely Adelaide would go to her father's employees – they would only take her back to the ranch, unless she had lied to him about the true state of her life. But why would she lead him all the way out to this remote spot and direct him to the rustled stock? She must have known she would implicate her brother in the rustling.

He looked for tracks as he rode in the direction he thought the valley entrance was situated, and two hours of steady riding brought him to where he expected it should be, but there was nothing to be seen. A solid rock wall rose up like an escarpment. He found no tracks. The stretches of dust lay undisturbed, except for the spoor of small wild animals. He sat his horse and subjected the area to a close scrutiny. Then he rode along the rock wall, studying it intently, until he came to a small waterfall that splashed down from a ledge much higher up. The water gushed into a pool directly beneath. The air around it was cool, and droplets of water were spread over a wide area like incessant rain.

Kelf rode closer to the pool and saw an area beyond and to the left which was littered with small rocks. His gaze pierced the mist like droplets splashing up from the pool and as his eyes adjusted to moist haze, he saw a cavern like opening at the back of the pool. He swung out of his saddle and led his horse into cover; drew his rifle from its scabbard, and went to the left of the pool and skirted the water. He was surprised to see there was space enough for several steers to advance shoulder to shoulder around the pool and into the cavern mouth, and he went forward eagerly to explore the mystery of Rainbow valley.

When he was directly behind the waterfall, he turned his back to it and gazed into the cave, which inclined slightly to a large circle of sunlight some fifty yards before him. He followed the tunnel and emerged into the valley, and a guard stepped into view with abrupt suddenness from behind a nearby rock and pointed a rifle at him.

'Who in hell are you, wandering around here like you owned the place?' the man demanded. He was tall and thin, dressed in stained range clothes, and his harshly-set face was showing surprise. 'I didn't hear you approach! Where's your horse? You're sneaking around, so who are you?'

'Willard Stratton sent me,' Kelf said unhesitatingly. 'His sister went missing from the ranch, and Willard thought she might have come up here. It's one of her favourite spots.'

'Yeah, she's here,' the man said. 'She rode in just before you. She said she's going to stay a few days.'

'I'll have to talk her and then report back to Willard,' Kelf said.

'You'd better fetch your horse then. It's a long ride to the shack in the valley. How long have you been riding for the Strattons? I ain't seen you around before.'

'I drifted into the ranch last week and Willard set me on. I'll get my horse.'

He retraced his steps, fetched his horse, and rode back to where the guard was waiting.

'There's a beaten path to the shack,' the guard said. 'Just follow it, and don't stray from it or one of the boys will put a slug through you.'

Kelf swung into his saddle and followed the path that meandered through clustered rocks. The valley opened up as he made progress, and he studied his surroundings intently as he left cover and traversed the open valley. He passed a herd of cattle, and saw that some of them were wearing his brother's brand. He pushed his horse into a lope and headed for the shack standing under a fringe of trees close to the creek.

He spotted a corral behind the shack which contained about ten horses, one of them being the palomino Adelaide Stratton had ridden from the ranch. He wondered if she would tell the rustlers who he really was, and dropped a hand to his gun butt.

Two men were standing by the corral, and they turned when they heard the sound of approaching hoof beats. When they saw that Kelf was a stranger they pulled their pistols and covered him.

'How in hell did you get in here?' The eldest of the pair, a short, fat man with cold blue eyes and a tight mouth, cocked his gun as Kelf reined in before them. 'I'm Ike Sullivan, the boss of this outfit. What's your handle?'

'I'm Charlie,' Kelf said briefly. 'Willard Stratton sent me to see if Adelaide is here. The guard told me she rode in a short while ago.'

'So you're riding nurse-maid on her, huh? Rather you than me. She's one helluva of a woman, but she acts like she's been eating loco weed. She's in the shack. I hope you're gonna get her out of my hair and take her back to the ranch.'

'That depends on her,' Kelf retorted. He rode to the shack, and glanced around before dismounting. Neither of the two men had followed him. He trailed

53

his reins and pushed open the door of the shack and came face to face with Adelaide. She smiled at him.

'I wondered if you would come here to check if I'd ridden in,' she said. 'Another man would have headed over the nearest crest to get away from me.'

'I said I'd get you to town, so if you've finished playing games then we'd better get moving. If these rustlers knew the truth about what we're doing there would be gun play, and some dead men. I'd like to avoid that kind of trouble right now.'

'If you get my horse from the corral I'll be ready to ride out with you,' she said.

'We're through playing games,' he said sternly. 'Come with me to the corral and I'll get your horse, but you stick close to me while we're in here.'

She shrugged and walked out of the door and he followed her. She led the way to the corral, and Kelf led his horse as he walked beside her. At the corral, he picked up a lariat looped around a post and climbed into the pen, shaking out the loop and moving forward to confront the palomino. The other horses ran to the far end of the corral but the palomino stood its ground, shaking its head.

'She's always been difficult to rope,' Adelaide told him. 'She's learned to dodge the loop.'

Kelf moved in, watching the horse intently. He made a feint with the rope, as if he was about to cast it, and the horse swung its head to its right, and then changed direction abruptly and ran in the direction Kelf threw the loop, which settled squarely over the animal's head and tightened around its sleek neck. Kelf went along the rope hand over hand, moving fast, and grasped the rope close to the palomino's neck. When he turned to the corral gate the horse walked meekly at his side.

Adelaide was waiting with a bridle, and she had a grin on her face. Kelf slipped the bridle over the horse's head, put the bit between the strong teeth, and buckled it. He wrapped the reins around a post, fetched the saddle, and a few moments later they were riding towards the entrance to the valley.

Kelf noticed Adelaide glancing around nervously. He was keeping an eye on their surroundings in case of trouble, and he was struck by the woman's manner. She was nervous where before she had been perfectly poised.

'What's wrong?' he demanded. 'What are you up to now? You're expecting something bad to happen, huh?'

'I'm thinking Willard will be here any time now,' she replied. 'Did you think I'd let you get the better of my family? They're not good by a long rope, but they're all I've got. When I came in, I told the guard to let you through but to stop you going out before Willard arrived, and I think I've timed it right. If I'm not mistaken there's dust at the entrance and riders are coming this way.'

Kelf drew his gun as he took in the situation. Adelaide laughed.

'You can't get away except by using the game trail

up the grey bluff in the left hand wall a mile or so past the shack. If you ride hell for leather you'll just about get up the trail before my brother and the men can stop you.'

'You've trapped me in here, and now you're showing me a way to escape?' he snapped.

'I've changed my mind. You seem a decent sort and you tried to help me despite your own problems. Now, you'd better get moving. That's Willard leading six men, and they are coming for you.'

Kelf looked towards the distant entrance to the valley, saw a number of riders coming in fast. He glanced around the entrance, saw no signs of cover at hand, and realized he had no choice but to trust Adelaide and hope that this time she was not lying. He swung his horse around and rode back towards the shack, moving in close to the left hand wall of the valley where there was some broken ground. He glanced over his right shoulder and saw Adelaide sitting her horse where he had left her, and the approaching riders were making good progress in his direction.

His sense of caution was overruled by the gravity of the situation and he pushed the horse to greater effort. Two men emerged from the shack as he rode by.

'What's going on?' one of them shouted.

'There's a posse coming into the valley,' Kelf said, and spurred his horse for greater effort.

He rode up valley, twisting his neck from time to

time to watch the progress of the following riders. He looked for the grey bluff and when he saw it ahead, he felt his hopes plummet. It was almost sheer, and he didn't think a horse could ascend it. But when he rode closer he saw that a great area of the rock wall had slid down into the valley, leaving a raw cleft from top to bottom – rough and dangerous, with loose shale at the foot. He set the black at the broken ground and the animal went at it determinedly.

Twice the animal almost lost its balance on the treacherous slope. Kelf leaned forward over the saddle horn, hauled on the reins, and lifted the horse's head up from the rocky ground. The animal staggered, its hoofs clattering on bare rock, and then began to drift sideways, fighting to maintain its balance. Kelf threw himself out of the saddle and ran in a crouch up the slope, looking for cover. The black ran back to level ground.

Kelf knew at that moment that he was finished. He could not ascend the gradient, and he could see his horse running across the valley. He drew his pistol and moved into the mass of broken rock littering the ground and lower slope. A Colt boomed and a bullet struck rock close to his head before screeching away in ricochet. He turned at bay, ready to sell his life dearly. The riders closed in like buzzards smelling blood.

He ducked into the cover of a rock the size of a barn that was teetering on the slope, disturbed by loose shale moving below it. A number of slugs smashed against the rock and whined into the distance. Kelf remained motionless, gun ready. The shooting eased and then petered out. He heard a heavy voice shouting, giving him an ultimatum. He heard a horse scrabbling on the uneven slope as one of the more daring of the riders tried to make progress.

Kelf eased to his right and took a one-eyed look around his cover. He saw Willard Stratton waiting in the background while his riders attacked the slope, with no more success than Kelf had found. The riders were firing again, and bullets thudded harmlessly against the rock. Kelf flattened out behind his cover and eased forward until he could see targets. He fired two shots in quick succession, and two of the riders vacated their saddles. The other four turned and rode back out of range.

Kelf thumbed back the brim of his Stetson and cuffed sweat from his forehead. He had given them something to think about. He took another look down the slope and saw Stratton gesticulating, shouting for his crew to make another attack. Kelf drew a bead on Stratton's chest and gently squeezed the trigger. The half-inch chunk of lead struck the big man squarely, the impact hurling him backwards out of his saddle. He hit the ground hard and rolled lifelessly. Kelf turned his gun on the other riders, and another pitched to the ground. The three survivors turned around and rode to a safer part of the valley. Kelf reloaded his empty gun with cartridges from the loops on his gun belt.

He emerged from his cover and made his way back to the valley floor, checking fallen riders as he went. Only one man was still alive, bleeding profusely. He went to Willard Stratton's side, found the man alive but unconscious with a bullet high in his chest. He quickly assessed the situation. With Willard in his hands he now held the upper hand, and did not waste any time. He fetched Stratton's horse and loaded the wounded man into the saddle, roping him in place with the lariat on the saddle horn. Then he looked around for his horse, and saw the animal grazing quietly a hundred yards away.

The animal came to him when he whistled, head held high to avoid stepping on its reins. Kelf prepared to travel. He checked his guns and tied the lead rope from Stratton's horse to his saddle horn. He mounted and rode back down the valley towards the shack, noting several riders moving around near the distant entrance. He passed the grazing herd and crossed over to the left hand side of the valley, saw men riding around to cut him off. He kept moving, confident that Stratton would be a big pawn to use in his dealings with the rustlers.

Adelaide emerged from the shack as he passed it. Her face was pale. When she recognized her brother, she came running towards Kelf, who reined in and sat watching his surroundings. Adelaide came up, staring in horror at her unconscious brother.

'Have you killed him?' she demanded in a quaking tone.

'He was alive when I put him across his saddle,' he replied. 'Most of his men are dead, and there'll be more corpses when I attempt to bust out of here. You might be able to save some of your crew by riding ahead and telling the guards that your brother needs a doctor bad, and I'll turn him loose for you to take care of the minute I get outside the valley. I want all those men down at the entrance to move inside the valley and put some distance between them and me. Get yourself a horse and do as I say, and the sooner I get out of here the sooner you can have Willard.'

She gazed at him for some moments before turning and running to the corral, where her palomino was tethered. Kelf watched her ride to the entrance, and after she spoke to the men there they all headed up valley. Adelaide remained at the entrance, and when the way was clear Kelf rode to join her, leading Willard Stratton.

'Get him down off the horse,' Adelaide said. 'I need to check him.'

'When I get clear of this place,' Kelf responded. 'You can ride with me until I'm out of gunshot range.'

'You're a hard man.' Adelaide shook her head. 'Willard could be bleeding to death while you're keeping him here.'

'I didn't ask him to attack me. His men were shooting to kill.' He twisted in his saddle to check the men who had ridden up the valley. They were in plain sight and out of shooting range. Before he could

60

straighten up he caught a quick movement out of a corner of his eye, and swung to meet trouble.

A man was leaping at him from a shelf in the rock wall, arms outstretched to drag him out of his saddle. He did not have time to react. The man landed on him, knocking him out of the saddle. He just had time to kick his feet clear of the stirrups before the man struck him. He hit the ground with an impact that drove the breath from his lungs. The man landed atop him, punching desperately with both hands, and all Kelf could do at that moment was pull in his chin and cover up.

The punches Kelf took were the hardest he had ever experienced. Hard knuckles smacked against his left temple and bright spots flashed across his vision. He rolled and arched his back, throwing off the man and starting to his feet. The man got up and reached for his pistol. Kelf made his play. His pistol seemed to spring into his hand and he fired, all in one fluid movement. The man jerked, his gun only half-drawn, and then he collapsed, his gun falling into the dust.

Kelf staggered as he got to his feet. He shook his head and his senses swirled. He dropped to one knee to save himself from falling and shook his head several times. When he was able to look up he saw Adelaide standing nearby, a pistol in her hand, the black hole of its muzzle gaping at him. Her taut face was a picture of extreme desperation.

His gun was still in his hand, but Kelf holstered it,

shaking his head. 'OK,' he said. 'I don't shoot women, so you've got the edge. Take your brother and start for town with him. I'll head out in another direction. Is it a deal?'

Adelaide's face was chalky white, her eyes filled with shock. 'Go on, get out of here,' she said. 'Move out before I kill you.'

Kelf looked into her face before turning away. He climbed into his saddle and rode out of the valley entrance. His sense of direction had him turning the head of his horse to Temple Rock, and there was just one thought in his mind. He needed some help now to retrieve the rustled stock and round up the rustlers.

He had large reserves of determination, and needed them on the long ride to Temple Rock. He retraced his trail until he reached his brother's ranch, and entered to take care of the needs of himself and his horse. The dead men had been removed from around the house but there were still signs that fighting had taken place. When he was ready to continue to town, the day was nearly over. Shadows were long on the sea of grass encompassing him. The sun had disappeared beyond the western horizon and stars were already twinkling in the sky. He rode steadily until he spotted the lights of Temple Rock and, as he kneed his horse forward into movement to enter the town, two riders confronted him from the shadows, starlight glinting on their drawn pistols.

'What's this, a hold up?' Kelf demanded.

'Not in the way you mean,' one of the men replied. 'We're posse men, and we have to check all arrivals. There's been trouble on the range. The sheriff was shot and a number of men were killed. We're looking for Stratton riders, so declare yourself. Who are you, mister, and where have you come from? I smell gun smoke on you, so where do you fit in with what's been going on around here?'

'Don't get excited,' Kelf said. 'I'm Brent Kelf. My brother is John Kelf of the Big K, and I was helping the deputy, Pete Carter, out at the Big K ranch when the sheriff was shot. Is Carter back in town? I need to talk to him, so point me in the right direction and I'll go about my business.'

'We've been told to watch for you, Kelf,' said the other posse man, kneeing his horse forward. 'If you'll follow me I'll take you straight to Carter.'

'Lead on,' said Kelf said, exhaustion clawing at his insides. It had been a long day, and he needed food and a bed. He followed his guide along the street, glancing around at the buildings and anonymous figures on the sidewalks. He heard the sound of a honky-tonk piano coming from a saloon; the batwings moving incessantly as men entered for their evening's entertainment. He moistened his lips. His throat was dry. His eyes felt as if their sockets were on fire. His left arm was throbbing just below the elbow where he had been creased by a slug. He needed to call it a day.

He was led to the front of the law office, and the posse man went back to his position outside town limits. Kelf dismounted, wrapped his reins around a hitching rail, and as he stepped up on to the sidewalk, a gun hammered twice in quick succession and orange muzzle flame spurted from the alley on the left of the law office. Kelf went down on one knee, his reflexes still razor sharp despite his tiredness. The shots passed him closely, and as he flattened out on the boardwalk, he drew his pistol and cocked it. . . .

FIVE

A faint tang of gun smoke came on the breeze to Kelf's nostrils. Gun echoes faded. He held his pistol ready, but there was no movement from the alley, and he began to suspect that his assailant had departed. The door of the law office was suddenly dragged open and a shaft of yellow lantern light bathed the boardwalk in front of it. A bulky figure filled the doorway.

'What in hell is going on out here?' the deputy called.

'Someone just took a shot at me from the alley on your left,' Kelf replied, and walked through the light to confront Carter. 'He fired one shot and then took off.'

'Kelf!' the deputy said in some surprise. 'I wasn't expecting to see you for days, if ever again. It didn't take you long to give up on those rustlers.'

'Give up?' Kelf pushed forward and entered the office as Carter stepped back. 'Do you know a place

65

called Rainbow Valley?'

'I've never heard of it.'

'Well, that's the place where the rustled cattle are being held.'

Kelf sat down at the lawman's desk and tried to relax. He explained tersely what had happened to him since they parted. Carter listened silently, his lips compressed and his eyes glinting.

'So that's the way of it, huh?' Carter mused when Kelf fell silent. 'I'll have a posse out at sunup and we'll take those thieves.'

'Sunup won't do,' Kelf said. 'A posse should set out immediately.'

'You look like you'll never make it back to that valley,' Carter said. 'Those steers won't be going anywhere, and it's obvious the Strattons are behind the rustling, so we can pick up the pieces later. I've met some opposition in town since I got in with my prisoners. Your family got here safely and they're staying at the freighter's place. Jeff Thompson is your sister-in-law's father, and he's got some tough men working for him. The sheriff is unable to do his job. He's out of it for a couple of months, and I'm waiting to hear from Clint Hanson, the mayor, whether or not the town council wants me to take over the sheriff's job until Denton is able to resume his duties.'

'I thought that would be a foregone conclusion,' Kelf said. 'That's what a deputy is for.'

'Not in this town.' Carter shook his head. 'Temple Rock is on Stratton range, and Abel Stratton owns most of the businesses here. His name is on every trading place in town, including the dress shop, which is run by his wife. If the Strattons are handling the rustling then we're stranded here with the enemy. I'm always hard put to get a posse together because most of the townsmen rely on Stratton for their wages. It's a bad situation, and there's no way around it.'

'You're not Stratton's man!'

'Stratton knows I'm not, and now the shooting has started I expect to be out of a job by morning. Stratton will have his own man in this office, and anyone who has taken part in this trouble against him will probably be run out of town. The shot that was just fired at you – I reckon it came from a Stratton gun. Do you see what we're up against?'

Kelf slumped in his seat. Tiredness was trembling through him. He looked into Carter's troubled eyes and shook his head. There was a limit to what a man could do, and he knew he had reached his boundary. He stood up wearily.

'I'm gonna find my brother and settle down for the night. Tomorrow is another day.'

'I'll walk you to the Thompson place,' Carter said. 'Come and look me up in the morning. If I've still got a job then we'll work something out.'

Kelf nodded and they left the office. Kelf led his horse, and his right hand was on the butt of his holstered pistol as they walked through the shadows. They entered an alley that was between a saloon and a store. A hanging lantern at the far end dimly illu-minated the shadowy corners. Kelf half expected shooting to erupt, but nothing happened, and they went on to the back lot, where lights showed the outline of a large house with a freight yard beyond.

'That's the freight depot,' Carter said. 'I'll leave you here. Thanks for your help earlier. I appreciate it. See you tomorrow.'

'Thanks,' Kelf replied. 'I hope you've still got a job in the morning.'

He went to the house, tied his horse to a rail, and heaved a sigh as he knocked on the front door. He watched the shadows until the door was opened by a powerful man who seemed as broad as he was long. He stared at Kelf with narrowed brown eyes, and grinned.

'No need for an introduction,' Jeff Thompson said. 'You look just like John. I'm pleased to meet you, Brent. John has just got through telling me what you did at the Big K earlier. We could do with a sheriff like you. Come in and make yourself to home. I'll take care of your horse shortly. Did you get a line on the rustlers?'

'I think that end of the trouble is pretty well tied down,' said Kelf as he entered the house. 'We can get the stock back, and deal with any of the rustlers who are sticking around.'

'Thanks for taking care of Josie and Billy on the trail. Those two are the light of my life. I'll be in your debt for the rest of my life.' Thompson opened a

68

door along the hall which ran the length of the house from the front to the back door, and Kelf saw John and his wife inside the big sitting room.

Josie sprang to her feet when she saw Brent, and came hurrying to his side. 'Are you OK?' she demanded. 'I've been worrying that you would have been shot to pieces by now. You shouldn't have gone alone.'

'Don't ever worry about me,' he responded. 'I did all right out there today.' He went to his brother's side, and John clasped his hand. 'Your stolen cows are in a place called Rainbow Valley. It's on Stratton range, and Willard Stratton at least is implicated in the rustling.'

'Are you hungry?' Josie cut in. 'I can get some food ready for you while you talk to John.'

'Those rustlers weren't in the mood for hospitality when I saw them.' Kelf grinned. 'The only item on the menu was hot lead, and there was plenty of that.' He sat down beside his brother and Josie left the room. 'I'll head out after your cattle in the morning,' he said. 'If the rustlers who survived our meeting moved the steers out they won't be able to travel more than twelve miles in twenty-four hours and we'll soon track them down.' He went on to explain the details of his day, and John grasped Brent's shoulder in shock when he learned that Willard Stratton was badly injured.

'That proves the Strattons are doing the rustling,' John said.

'What I don't understand is Adelaide Stratton's part in this business,' Brent said. 'She acts like she eats loco weed some of the time, and I was glad to get away from her. At one time I thought she would shoot me in cold blood. I left her to bring Willard into town to see the doc. The law can arrest him. On the other hand, she told me the steers were in Rainbow Valley, and showed me where it was when she learned I was a stranger around here.'

'I wish I was fit enough to sit a horse,' John said. 'I'd like nothing better than to face the sidewinders who have been giving us all the trouble.'

Josie returned, and Brent swallowed with an effort when he saw she was carrying a tall glass of beer.

'Could you do with this?' she asked, and Brent took it from her and drained it in a long gulp.

'I'm doing you a beef steak with all the trimmings,' Josie said, and left the room again.

Brent tried to relax. He leaned back in his chair, closed his eyes and allowed his mind to drift. Tiredness claimed him. He knew nothing more until Josie called his name, and he awoke to find a meal had been set on a table.

'It's a shame to wake you,' she said. 'But you'll sleep better with a full stomach. Come and eat your meal and I'll get a bed ready for you upstairs.'

'I won't sleep in the house,' Kelf said instantly. 'Someone took a shot at me from the alley beside the jail as I rode in, and there'll be other attempts, I expect. I can't afford to relax.'

'Where will you sleep?' Josie demanded.

'There'll be a barn outside. I'm used to sleeping rough. I've got my blankets on my horse and there's nothing else I need. If anyone is out to get me then I'd better stay away from my family. I don't want you caught up in any violence.'

He ate the meal, thanked Josie for her efforts, and was on the point of getting to his feet when Jeff Thompson entered the room. The big freighter was carrying a double-barrelled 12 gauge shot gun, and his expression was serious.

'I've been watching my freight yard,' he said, 'and I saw a figure sneaking in over a wall. I've had some trouble lately.' He looked at Brent. 'Would you back me while I take a look around?'

Brent got to his feet, his tiredness evaporating quickly. 'Lead the way,' he said instantly, and Josie uttered a gasp as they left the room.

Thompson went out of the back door, followed closely by Brent. Several lanterns were strung up around the big yard, creating pools of brilliant light counter-balanced by many dark shadows. Bob-wire was strung around the outer wall, which surrounded the yard without break, except for a heavy gate that was intricately wired.

'I heard a noise over there.' Kelf pointed to a low building across the yard.

'Yeah, I heard it. That's the stable. I guess one of the horses is restless, or someone is prowling around and making it uneasy.' Thompson walked across the yard and inched open the stable door. Kelf remained close by the freighter's side, holding his pistol in his right hand. The silence was intense. Somewhere along the main street a piano was being played, the sound echoing eerily in the distance, and Kelf thought of the men in town who had nothing to do but enjoy their free time.

Thompson entered the stable and Kelf went with him. There was no light inside and the darkness was so intense Kelf imagined he could carve his initials on it. The freighter leaned in against Kelf and whispered, 'I know where the lantern is. You stand ready and I'll strike a match.'

Kelf cocked his gun and crouched. Thompson moved several yards away, making little sound for someone of his bulk. A match scraped and flared, and Kelf peered around as brightness filled the stable. He saw a figure standing at the far end of the building, holding a can in one hand and a pistol in the other. A second figure was standing in an inner doorway, and Kelf caught sight of a flickering light behind the second man.

At that moment all hell broke loose. Both interlopers began shooting. The stable was filled with gun thunder and spurting muzzle flame. Kelf flowed into action with his customary speed, firing a shot before his gun barely cleared its holster, and the nearest man, holding the can, was hit as he fired his first shot. He jerked and buckled at the knees, struck dead centre by Kelf's deadly shooting. Wreathed in gun smoke, his gun spilled from his hand and he sprawled on the ground, jerking spasmodically. Thompson stepped forward level with Kelf, thrust his shot gun forward, and squeezed the trigger. The long gun blasted with a noise like a cannon, and the second man seemed to fade away, blood spurting from multiple wounds caused by the whirling load of buckshot, going down like a leaf blown in a storm.

Kelf looked around. All he could see was fire burning in the end room. He ran forward, holstering his pistol, and dragged the fallen man out of the doorway. He snatched a horse blanket off a rail and began beating at the spreading fire, amazed at how fast the writhing tendrils of flame were igniting the straw. Thompson joined him and they flailed the fire with smoke broiling around them.

The sound of a gun blasted outside the stable. Thompson ran to the door, thrust it open, and was met by a volley of shots. He turned away from the door, losing his grip on the shotgun, and staggered a couple of steps towards Kelf before dropping to his knees and falling on his face.

Kelf stared at the freighter. He dared not stop fighting the blaze for he was aware that fire was the biggest threat to a townsman. He swung the horse blanket, beating at the straw, half-blinded by smoke and sweat, and cast a look over his shoulder towards the door when he heard it being dragged open. Josie appeared, and whatever she intended to do she gasped in horror at the sight of her father lying on the ground and fell on her knees beside him.

The fire was abating, the flames decreasing. Kelf swung the blanket like a madman, advancing step by step, and he dropped to his knees, exhausted, when he realized he had overcome the conflagration. He gasped for breath but only succeeded in filling his lungs with smoke. He staggered to his feet and reeled to the door, where Josie was examining Thompson's wound.

'Is he badly hurt?' Kelf demanded.

Josie looked up at him, her face set in a mask on shock and anxiety. She shook her head in answer to his question.

'Did you see any strangers in the yard as you came from the house?' Kelf persisted.

She shook her head again. Kelf drew his gun and went to the door. He dragged it open and several shots came snarling into the stable, thudding into the surrounding woodwork, clanging against metal. Several horses were tethered in stalls, and they were pulling at their halters and stamping their feet in panic. Kelf dropped to one knee by the doorway, thrust his gun forward, and began to shoot at the gun flashes splitting the shadows.

In a matter of moments the opposition diminished against him. The blasting guns fell silent and echoes began to fade. Josie came to Kelf's side and touched his shoulder. He pulled her down instantly, moved back from the doorway, and eased her out of harm's way.

'My dad is badly hurt, Brent,' she said, her face ashen in the lamp light. 'Can you get him into the house while I fetch the doctor?'

'We'll put him in the house and go for the doctor together,' he replied. 'You can't go off by yourself while there is shooting. Take my gun, and fire shots if there is resistance. It doesn't matter if you don't hit anyone. Just keep their heads down. I'll carry your dad out of here.'

She took his gun. Kelf lifted Thompson, who was semi-conscious, and half carried him to the door. The freighter's feet moved sluggishly and they made slow progress across the yard. There was no more shooting. Josie was waving his gun around as if it was a flag on Independence Day. They gained the house, entered, and Josie bolted the back door. She led the way to the room where John Kelf was waiting, a gun in his hand and frustration showing on his face.

John was full of questions. Brent examined Thompson and decided that he was not seriously wounded.

'Tell me where the doctor lives and I'll fetch him,' he said. 'Don't worry, Josie, your dad will survive. I reckon he'll be up on his feet again in a matter of weeks. One thing I do know about is bullet wounds.'

'Doc Farrell's house is on Main Street next to the dress shop,' Josie said. Her eyes were large and showed the horror she was feeling. 'Go along the alley to Main Street and turn left. You'll see a name-plate on the doctor's wall by the front door.'

Kelf left the house and walked along the alley to the main street. He was carrying his gun in his hand, but had no trouble. He found the doctor's house and knocked at the door, turning to survey his surroundings until it opened.

Doc Farrell was in his fifties, a short, fleshy-faced man who looked as if he had the cares of the town written into the lines on his face. He was medium sized, and his blue eyes contained an analytical expression that seemed to proclaim that he knew everything there was to know about his fellowmen and their way of life.

'Doc, there's been some shooting at the freight depot and Jeff Thompson is wounded. Can you come now?'

The doctor turned instantly to a table in his hall and picked up a medical bag.

'Let's go,' he said.

They walked back along the street, and Kelf gave the doctor details of the shooting.

'I don't know what the world is coming to,' Farrell said, shaking his head. 'There's nothing but shooting and killing going on day and night. It's about time the town council increased the number of lawmen around here. I've voted for the motion several times, but some of these businessmen believe it would be wasting money. This town is owned by Abe Stratton, and he has a big say in what will be done. Who shot Thompson?'

'I don't know. He saw someone climbing over the

wall into his freight yard, and I went with him to look around. A couple of men had got in and were setting fire to the stable. We managed to put out the fire, and then more men attacked the place and Jeff took a bullet in the chest.'

'And who are you? I haven't seen you before.'

'I'm Brent Kelf. My brother is John Kelf of Big K. I'm on a visit from Kansas.'

They reached the Thompson house. Farrell attended to his patient, aided by a tearful Josie, and announced that Thompson's life was not in danger, barring further accidents and infection. Brent helped the doctor carry Thompson up to his bedroom and they made him comfortable.

'You saw Sheriff Denton today, didn't you?' Kelf asked the doctor.

'You've met our sheriff?' Farrell countered.

Kelf explained the details, and Farrell shook his head.

'The sheriff will live, but he won't be wearing his law badge for several months. From what I know of the situation around here, I'd say that you are up to your neck in trouble. Your brother is on Stratton's black list. They're already giving him trouble to put him out of business, and now they've started on Jeff Thompson. He's about the only businessman around here who is not in Stratton's pocket, so the attack tonight shows that they're beginning the process of getting rid of him.'

'That's the way I figure it,' Kelf said. 'Will you let

me know if you're called to anyone wearing a bullet hole, Doc? I need to put faces and names to any of the men involved in the shooting around here this evening.'

'I'll pass the word to the deputy,' Farrell told him. 'But don't get too hopeful. Half the men in town work for the Strattons in one way or another, and what they say goes, even to the extent of murder. As a doctor I've got much closer to this community, and I've heard some strange facts from men who have suffered violence for no apparent reason. It always comes back to the Strattons. It was bad enough before Willard Stratton was old enough to actively help his father, but now he's full grown he's adding his own nastiness to the business.'

'I've met Willard, and his father, and I'd say at a guess that someone will have to kill them to stop them.'

'And you're ready to go that far?' Farrell asked.

Kelf shrugged. 'I don't have an alternative, Doc. If I don't stop them they are going to kill my brother.'

The doctor nodded and departed. Kelf went out to the yard to check around. He repaired a couple of holes in the wire fence, looked in every dark corner, and was satisfied that no interlopers remained. He checked the horses, settling down again after their fright in the fire, and went back into the house to settle in a store room at the back of the house to get some sleep.

Despite his tiredness he slept fitfully, getting up

twice in the night to check around. He was not fooled by the quietness. It was just the calm before the storm. He could only hope that his luck would hold to the final shoot-out.

SIX

Kelf was standing in a corner of the yard as the sun came up the next morning. The crucial time of waiting for dawn passed without incident. When there was enough light to see clearly he went around the yard to check, and picked up a discarded black Stetson which had a rattlesnake skin for a hat band. The initials DR were inked inside the hat. He went into the house and saw Josie, whose face was showing worry and fear.

'I'm sorry I got you to leave Kansas, Brent,' she said. 'This trouble had nothing to do with you, and I feel responsible for bringing you into it.'

'You're kin,' he replied, 'and if my brother and his wife are in trouble then this is the place for me. Don't worry, Josie. It'll all come right in the end. Take a look at this hat. I found it in the yard. One of the men must have dropped it last night. Note the rattle skin hat band. Have you seen anyone wearing it around town? The initials DR are on the inside band.'

'DR!' Josie said, frowning. 'Those initials should be easy to trace.'

'Think about it,' he suggested. 'I'll have a word with John.' He paused, and then said, 'How is your father this morning?'

Her eyes clouded, but she made a brave attempt to smile. 'He's making progress, and told me he wants to talk to you as soon as you're ready.'

John was already down in the sitting room, and greeted Brent with enthusiasm.

'What are your plans for today, Brent?' he asked.

'In view of what I learned about the rustlers yesterday, I reckon to go out and grab Abel Stratton and bring him in for Carter to arrest and charge. I figure that as Willard Stratton is guilty then his father must be in on the rustling. Willard is being brought in to see the doctor. Carter will jail him on my evidence, and if I can get Abel then the rest of their outfit will have no leaders and be easier for the law to handle.'

'You can't go out to the AS ranch without some backing,' John said. 'You'll only get yourself killed, and I don't know where you'll get gun help from around here.'

'If I play my cards right there won't be any need for gun play,' Brent said. 'Just leave it to me, John. Now look at this hat. I picked it up in the yard just now. One of the men doing the shooting here last night must have lost it.'

81

John took the hat and examined it. After a few moments he looked up at Brent. 'I know who this belongs to,' he said harshly. 'It's Dogie Roberts. He works with his father running the livery barn. He's a Stratton man. The Strattons own the business. What are you gonna do about this, Brent?'

'I'll have a bite to eat, talk to your father-in-law, and then brace Roberts.'

After breakfast Brent went up to Jeff Thompson's bedroom. The freighter lay on his bed, in considerable pain. He was sweating and restless, breathing heavily, and there was a hint of fever in his eyes. But he grinned weakly and held up a hand for Brent to shake.

'I sure owe you a bundle of thanks,' he said.

'Don't worry about a thing,' Kelf told him. 'Everything is OK around the yard. The fire didn't do much damage. We jumped on it quickly enough to control it. After you were shot, I fixed a couple of places in the wire where the trouble-makers got through, and I was alert most of the night, which was quiet.'

'I've got a dozen good men working for me and they'll want to fight this trouble. I reckon a couple of them should remain around here in case there is another attack and the rest can ride with you. The freighting business will cease until we've beaten the Strattons. How does that sound?'

'It's pretty good. I'm going to see the deputy shortly and get his view on what should be done and we'll ride out and get on with it. If we act fast, we'll clean up before the Strattons know what's going on.'

'I've sent word to my yard foreman to come and see me,' Thompson went on. 'Lem Tolliver is a mighty tough man, and as straight as a rail. You two should get on well. Wait around until you can meet him.'

'I'd hate to have help from men who might be killed,' Kelf said.

'They'll be fighting for me, their jobs and their future,' Thompson said. 'Don't worry about it.' He paused, studied Kelf's face for a few moments, and then asked, 'What will you do when this trouble is over?'

Kelf smiled and shook his head. 'That sounds like tempting Fate. I'll wait until it's done before I decide.'

A heavy hand rapped on the door panel and it was opened by a large man who filled the doorway and had to bend his head to look inside the room. Everything about him was bigger than average; his head was large, and covered with red hair. His blue eyes were narrowed behind a long nose, and his thin-lipped mouth was set above a prominent chin that looked as if it had been chopped out of granite. His body, arms and legs were massive, his hands the biggest Kelf had ever seen. His eyes settled on Kelf and hardened, a smile on his face vanishing as he instinctively dropped his big right hand to his holster. Thompson stopped the movement by calling an introduction.

'Lem, I want you to meet John Kelf's brother Brent. He only showed up two days ago but he's played hell with the rustlers. On top of that, he was here last evening when some bad men showed up. They fired the stable, and died where they stood. I got a slug in my chest, and Brent chased off some others who were bent on more trouble. So as from now, I'm halting all freighting until this trouble has been smashed, and I want you and the men to work with Brent.'

'OK, boss!' Lem held out a great hand for Kelf to shake. 'Anything you say. I'll talk to the men when they report for work.'

'I reckon two of them should stick around here to guard the property while the rest act as a posse under Brent's control. He seems to be doing all the right things. They've got to stomp the bad men causing this trouble.'

'That sounds good, boss.' Tolliver grinned. 'I'll ride with Brent.'

'I'll be glad to have you along,' Kelf told him. 'I've got some business to handle now and then I have to check with the deputy, then I'll be ready to ride.'

'We'll be ready and loaded for bear when you get back,' Tolliver told him.

Kelf left the house, taking the black Stetson with him, and walked along the street to the livery barn. The town was on the move. A man wearing a white apron was sweeping the boardwalk in front of the general store. A woman was cleaning the windows of the dress shop. She paused and stared at Kelf as he passed her, frowning as she studied him, and when he was almost a pace or so past her she called to him.

'What are you doing with Dogie Roberts's hat?'

'I'm on my way to give it back to him,' Kelf said.

'How did you get it from him?'

'He dropped it in the dark last night and couldn't find it.'

'He never goes anywhere without that hat.'

'Then I must hurry to return it to him.' Kelf touched his hat and continued along the sidewalk.

A wagon was outside the front of the livery barn, loaded with straw, and the hay loft door was open. An old man was standing in the doorway of the loft with a pitch fork in his hands. A man standing on the top of the load of straw was tossing baled straw into the loft and the man inside was clearing it away.

'Howdy,' Kelf called. 'I'm looking for Dogie Roberts.' He held up the hat. 'I've been told this hat belongs to him. Is he here?'

'I'm his father,' said the man in the loft doorway. 'Dogie ain't here this morning. He fell sick last night. Leave the hat inside in my office and I'll return it to him.'

'I'd like to return it to him personally,' Kelf insisted. 'Where can I find him?'

'My house is across the street. It's the one with the white picket fence. My wife is there. Dogie is in bed.'

'What's wrong with him?'

'My wife's got no idea. I reckon she'll have Doc Farrell in later to look at him.'

Kelf crossed the street. He found the house with the white picket fence and knocked at the front door. A small woman wearing an apron answered. She had a worried face and looked at Kelf is if she afraid that he would bite her.

'Are you the man Dogie had trouble with last night?' she demanded.

'No, ma'am. I didn't have trouble with anyone last night. I found this hat, was told it belonged to your son, and I've brought it right along to return it.'

'That's good of you. Dogie said someone stole it from him last night.'

'Can I see Dogie? I'm sure he'd wanta thank me for taking the trouble to bring the hat back.'

'He's ill.' Mrs Roberts shook her head. 'I'll tell him you've returned it and I'm sure he'll look you up later to thank you.'

'Is he in bed?'

'He can't see you. I told you he's ill.' Her attitude changed as she spoke. She pursed her lips and started to close the door. Kelf put out his left hand to prevent the door closing. She tried to resist but could not match his strength and he held the door open.

'I'll forgive you for lying to me,' he said. 'You are his mother and bound to protect him. But I have to talk to him so tell me where he is.'

'He left the house early this morning. He said to tell any caller that he was ill. Is he in trouble? Are you

86

a lawman?'

Kelf shook his head. He stepped into the house and Mrs Roberts backed away from him. She glanced over her shoulder.

'Dogie,' she called. 'You'd better come out here and see this man. He's brought your hat back.'

Kelf heard a clatter close by, as if someone had overturned a chair in his haste to move out. An inner door slammed and heavy footsteps thudded. Kelf stepped around Mrs Roberts and ran along the passage that led to the back door. He jerked the door open and a gun blasted outside, tossing a bullet into the wooden panel beside Kelf's head. He ducked and peered out. A man holding a smoking pistol was turning to run away across the back lot. Kelf drew his gun and fired in a single, fluid-like movement, aiming for the man's right leg.

The man dropped his gun and went to ground in a sprawling fall, his leg suddenly useless. He squirmed around and tried to snatch up his gun. Kelf fired again, the shot sounding crisp in the early morning. The fallen gun jumped a couple of feet, and Dogie Roberts changed his mind and grasped his bleeding leg with both hands. Kelf approached him, the muzzle of his gun pointing at Roberts's heart.

Roberts was little more than a youth, thin and under-sized. His face was contorted with pain and he gazed at Kelf, his hands coming up before his chest as if preparing to ward off the next shot.

'You must have a guilty conscience,' Kelf said, holstering his gun and picking up the one Roberts had dropped. 'I found your hat in the freight yard this morning, heard that it belonged to you, and came to return it. Why did you shoot Jeff Thompson? He was hit in the chest and is seriously hurt.'

'I didn't shoot him,' Roberts protested.

'So who did?'

'I can't say. It would be more than my life is worth. I don't know anything.'

'Someone must have told you to join the men who fired Thompson's stable. Give me his name and I'll be satisfied.'

Roberts shook his head. He was whimpering in pain, and clutched his leg again. Kelf bent over him and examined his leg.

'It's not too bad,' he observed. 'Get up and I'll take you along to the law office. The deputy will handle you.'

'I can't stand,' Roberts protested.

Kelf secured a hold on Robert's collar and hauled him to his feet. Roberts offered no resistance and Kelf took him back into the house. Mrs Roberts was standing just inside the back door, her hands to her face, her shoulders shaking. Kelf thrust Roberts toward the front door and took him out to the street. He paused just outside, for the livery man and two others were standing by the gate. All three were holding weapons – Dogie's father grasped a shot gun.

88

'What's going on?' demanded Roberts. 'What are you doing with Dogie?'

Kelf explained tersely. He was holding Dogie's shirt collar with his left hand, his .45 gripped in his right hand. When he said he was John Kelf's brother, the three men exchanged glances, and the shot gun pointed its twin muzzles in his direction.

'Be careful what you do with the shotgun,' Kelf said quietly. 'If you fire it while your son is beside me you'll probably kill both of us. I'm sure you won't want that to happen so why don't you put down the gun and listen to reason? That goes for the two men with you. If any of you are still armed when I've finished talking then I'll start shooting, and it will be a free for all.'

Roberts considered for a moment and then lowered his gun. The other two did the same, and then one of them threw his weapon into the dust.

'Is it OK for me to walk away from this?' he asked.

'Sure,' Kelf said. 'Just turn your back and get to hell out of here. Your pard can do the same. This is a family affair so butt out.'

Both men turned and departed. They crossed the street and entered the livery barn. Kelf pulled Dogie back into the house before the two men could change their minds and get fresh guns.

'Come in, Mr Roberts,' Kelf invited. 'We've got some talking to do.'

The livery man obeyed, and Kelf closed the door with a sigh of relief. Roberts grabbed Dogie as he began to fall. Kelf holstered his gun and caught Dogie. They carried him to a couch in the front room, and Roberts called for his wife. She came into the room reluctantly, but when she saw the blood on Dogie's leg she overcame her fears.

'I'll get a bowl of water and a bandage,' she muttered, and scurried out. When she returned she busied herself with Dogie's wound.

'I could have killed him,' Kelf said. 'He started shooting at me.'

'What's Dogie done?' Roberts demanded.

Kelf recounted what had happened the previous evening, and saw that Roberts became uneasy.

'I know this is Stratton's town and the men in it who work for him are expected to look after Stratton's interests,' Kelf said. 'So Dogie took part in the raid on Jeff Thompson's freight yard. Thompson was seriously hurt and there was some damage to the yard. I expect you know exactly what happened, Roberts. Do you own the livery barn or are you running it for Stratton?'

'I did own it at one time, but I had to sell it to Stratton. What are you going to do about Dogie? Will he be jailed for being at Thompson's yard last night?'

'I don't know. That will be up to the deputy. What's the situation in town? Has Stratton taken control?'

'Yeah, our lives are not our own. If Stratton says jump, we jump. If he says he doesn't like someone new to the town then we freeze him out, or he meets with an accident.'

'So what happened to Thompson? He's been running that freight line for years.'

'Willard Stratton took a liking to the business, so Thompson has to go.'

'Where does the law stand in this?'

'Denton is Stratton's man. Stratton got him elected, and Denton does everything Stratton tells him.'

'And where does Carter stand?'

'There's talk that Stratton is not happy about him. He'll probably be the next to get the treatment.'

Kelf prepared to leave. He went to the door and paused, looking back. Mrs Roberts was bent over Dogie, bandaging his leg. Her face was turned towards Kelf, her expression harsh, filled with foreboding. Kelf felt sorry for her. He looked at Roberts, and the older man sat with slumped shoulders, defeat showing clearly in his weather-beaten face.

'Is there a boss man in town who runs things for Stratton?' Kelf asked. 'Who gave the orders last night for Dogie to attack the freight yard?'

'If it gets out that I told you anything then my life won't be worth a plugged nickel.' Roberts shook his head. 'But I can see now that we can't live like this any longer; our lives being run for us by ruthless men. Stratton has a stranglehold on the whole community. It can't go on. Sheriff Denton is the boss man around here for Stratton. He's the law, but he's guilty of just about every crime in the book. Put him out of business and Stratton won't be able to operate around here.'

Kelf departed and went to the law office. The door stood open and Carter was leaning in the doorway, gazing moodily around the street. The deputy grinned when he saw Kelf but he did not look happy.

'Have you got trouble?' Kelf demanded.

'I've been ordered to stick around here until the big men of the town decide what should be done,' Carter said in a bitter tone. 'I'm tempted to turn in this tin star, forget the petty rules, and go along with you to smash the rustlers for good.'

'You better stay put and look after things around here,' Kelf advised. 'I'll have several good men to ride with me when I leave, which I aim to do shortly, and we'll get things rolling.'

'You need a lawman with you,' Carter said.

'I think we can manage without one. But the town needs a good lawman. Have you got Willard Stratton in jail?'

'I ain't seen hide or hair of him or his sister Adelaide. She lied to you, Kelf. She didn't have any intention of bringing him to the jail.'

'They won't get far,' Kelf retorted. He decided not to tell Carter about what he had learned from Roberts. 'It's time I set out,' he said. 'I'll see you when I get back.'

Carter nodded, his lips twisting. 'If I get the word to carry on in Sheriff Denton's boots, I'll form a posse and come out to join you.'

Kelf wasted no more time. He went back to the Thompson house and prepared to ride out. He met the men who were to ride with him, and shook hands all round. They were men who had roughed it in a tough job and were prepared to risk their lives for the community. Kelf saddled his mount and waited for the others to finish their preparations for leaving. They were a motley bunch, heavily armed and, led by big Lem Tolliver, showed an appearance of determination and aggression.

Josie came to the door as the men were mounting. She called to Kelf.

'John would like to talk to you, Brent,' she said.

He dismounted and went into the house. John was keeping Billy amused, but looked apprehensive.

'I wish I was going with you,' he said.

'We'll manage without you,' Kelf told him. 'We're gonna get the herd back, and I hope the rustlers will try to stop us and that we'll be strong enough to hold them and wipe them out. If we win the game then I'll go along to the AS ranch and grab Abel Stratton.'

'That sounds good, but don't take any chances out there. The Strattons have about thirty men on their payroll, and if they catch you in the open you won't stand a chance.'

'That's good advice, John. Is there anything else?' Kelf was eager to be on the move.

'See you when you get back,' John said, shaking his head.

Kelf went out to his horse and swung into the

saddle. He led the party of six men. Tolliver rode at his side. Townsfolk paused on the sidewalks to watch them pass, and Kelf wondered how many of them were in cahoots with the rustlers. He noticed that most of the businesses in town had the Stratton name prominently displayed over their doorways. When he saw a gun shop along the street, he reined in at its hitch rail and stepped down from his saddle. It also had Stratton's name on it.

'I need to top up my supply of cartridges,' he said.

'We're lucky,' Tolliver replied. 'The boss told us to load up from the stuff we've got in our warehouse. We could start a war if you wanted to.'

Kelf entered the gun shop and a tall, lean man came out of a room at the back. There was no welcome on his face, and he eyed Kelf with suspicion glimmering in his dark eyes.

'Two boxes of .45s and a box of Winchester 44-40s,' Kelf said.

'You're a stranger in town,' the man observed. He was wearing a white apron over his clothes. He shook his head. 'I ain't seen you around before. Are you new in town?'

'I am. Give me the shells I asked for. I'm in a hurry.'

'Are you John Kelf's brother from Kansas? I heard you look a lot like him.'

'My name is Brent Kelf. John is my brother, and I've come from Kansas to help him fight this trouble he's getting. Now give me the shells. I've got a lot of riding to do today.'

'I hear you did a lot of riding yesterday,' the man countered.

'You hear too damn much,' Kelf retorted. 'I don't like your attitude, mister. Are you here to sell your stock or turn trade away? Get the shells for me or I'll take them.'

'It would be unwise of you to try. I've been told not to serve anyone who's lined up with John Kelf or his father-in-law, Jeff Thompson.' As he spoke, the man reached a hand under his counter, his eyes on Kelf's face. Kelf drew his gun and cocked it under the man's nose before he could bring a weapon into play.

'Don't let's get nasty over a few boxes of shells,' Kelf said harshly. 'Bring your hand back into the open, and it better not be holding a gun.'

The sound of a weapon hitting a shelf under the counter preceded the withdrawal of the man's hand, and his face was impassive as he raised his hands shoulder high.

'I don't have to serve you,' he said. 'And if you take anything out this shop without my permission you'll be stealing, even if you leave money for it.'

'Keep your mouth shut and get me the shells I asked for,' Kelf told him. He felt in his left-hand jacket pocket, produced a thin sheaf of greenbacks and peeled some off. He laid them on the counter, his hard gaze holding the man's aggressive stare.

The man lowered his hands and picked up three boxes of shells from a back shelf. He placed them before Kelf, took the money and gave Kelf the change.

'I heard you were greased lightning on the draw,' he said slowly, 'but they lied. You're hell on wheels, Kelf.'

'And don't forget it,' Kelf replied.

He went outside and put the boxes of cartridges in a saddle bag. Lem Tolliver was in his saddle, holding his pistol. He was smiling grimly.

'That little runt, Ossie Leavold, just made a gesture with his gun,' he said. 'He's a Stratton man, always poking around town and asking questions. When I drew my gun he dived into the barber's shop.'

'We'll clean up the town when we've handled the big job,' Kelf said. 'Let's get out of here and start what we've got to do.'

They rode along the street, watched by many peering eyes. When they hit the trail out of town, Kelf set the pace with a mile-eating lope and they settled down to a long ride. Two hours later, they reached Stratton range, and Kelf tensed as they continued. He was afraid of being caught flat-footed on AS grass, and when they approached a rise he halted.

'We must go carefully,' he said. 'After yesterday they'll be expecting trouble.'

Even as he spoke a burst of gun fire erupted from the top of the rise and gun smoke drifted. Lem Tolliver gave a great cry and toppled out of his saddle. Kelf felt the burn of a bullet across his left hip and wheeled his horse, jumping it into cover in a long depression. Two of the remaining men vacated their saddles and lay unmoving in the grass. The remaining four scrambled into the scant cover with Kelf.

SEVEN

Kelf sprang from his saddle and trailed his reins. He grabbed his Winchester from its boot and ascended the side of the depression, threw himself flat. He saw heads and shoulders on the crest above and lifted his rifle. Slugs were thudding into the ground around his position but he concentrated on action. He fired two shots at fleeting targets, saw a man fall back as a bullet struck home, and then settled down to a steady fight. He paused to urge his four surviving men to start replying to the gun fire, and one of them stood up to look for a target and was struck down instantly by accurate fire from above. The others ducked and stayed down.

Kelf knew their position was untenable. He slid back to his horse, mounted, and paused to call to the cowering men.

'We can't stay here,' he shouted. 'Let's get moving. Follow me and we'll attack them from the left.'

He dug in his spurs and his horse sprang forward,

leaving cover. Kelf kneed it to the left with crackling bullets following him. His hunched his body to minimize his target area and rode hell for leather, his rifle clasped in his right hand. He reached a sprawl of rocks some fifty yards to his right and dismounted in their cover. When he looked around for his men, he saw them riding fast downhill, back the way they had come and looking as if they would not stop until they reached town. He swung his gaze towards the position of their attackers, and saw four riders coming down from the crest, making for the spot where he was waiting, their guns blasting as they endeavoured to swamp him with fire.

Kelf dismounted and trailed his reins. He moved forward slightly to bring the attackers under his rifle and prepared for action. The men were in an irregular line about sixty yards above him. Kelf lifted his rifle to his shoulder, his eyes narrowed. He looked through his sights and centred on the nearest rider, moving his rifle to keep his aim ahead of the man. He fired, and the crack of the shot sent echoes fleeing across the range. The man wilted in his saddle until the starch ran out of him. Then he leaned forward, his rifle falling from his hands. He drooped over his saddle horn before pitching sideways and falling to the ground.

The other three riders continued as if they were on a ride to town on a Saturday. Kelf settled down and tossed lead at them, warming to the action. It was like shooting fish in a barrel. He fired three shots at the easy targets and three men went down. Kelf went back to his horse and mounted, continued to his left, aware that the volume of shooting coming from the crest had diminished considerably. He ascended the slope on a diagonal line, following a gully that gave him some protection from desultory fire.

Silence had fallen by the time he reached the crest. He thrust his rifle into its boot and drew his pistol. A party of four riders was heading away from the crest and he followed them, determined to cut them down. They reached fresh cover and turned at bay, shooting furiously as he sought cover. When he returned fire one of their guns fell silent and the rest pulled out.

Kelf was determined to overcome them but they were not inclined to stand against him, aware of his gun prowess. They rode on and did not halt again. Kelf reined in and watched them go. He was in no position to continue alone, and returned to the spot where they had been ambushed. When he reached it, he saw three of his party lying motionless under the blazing sun. Lem Tolliver was stretched out, arms out flung, face turned up to the brassy sky. His eyes were wide and glassy. A big patch of blood stained his shirt front. The other two men were dead also.

Kelf rounded up their horses and loaded the bodies on them, roping them in position. He started back to town, aware of the enormity of what he was trying to do. He knew he had no chance in an open confrontation because he was badly outnumbered. His only hope of success was to attack his enemies piecemeal.

By the time he sighted the town he had revised his plan. He had to strike fast at the men who were responsible for the grim situation affecting the range.

Main Street was crowded with folk, most of them gathered in groups, and all discussing the news that the deserters from Kelf's party had brought in on their return. When Kelf was spotted leading dead men draped over their saddles, a silence fell around the street. Kelf continued to the law office and the crowd followed him.

Carter was standing in his doorway, his craggy face expressionless. He shook his head when he met Kelf's gaze.

'Your posse ran out on you,' he observed. 'It takes a good man to stand up to ambush the first time he faces it. Did you get a look at any of the dry gulchers?'

Kelf shook his head. 'I'll be riding out alone shortly, and I'll have better luck,' he replied.

Carter nodded. 'I'll clean up this mess,' he said.

'One thing I learned this morning is that Sheriff Denton is running things around here for the Strattons. Have you got any proof of that?' He looked into the deputy's eyes. Carter did not flinch. 'If you got the deadwood on him it would be a lot easier for us to handle the rest of it.'

'I've had my suspicions about him, but he plays his cards close to his vest.'

'Where is he? He was brought back to town from my brother's spread. He was shot by one of Stratton's men.'

'He wasn't badly hurt. The doc has got him in a room in his house – reckons he'll be on his feet in a week or so. If I could get proof against him and put him behind bars my job would be a lot easier.'

'I'll have a talk with him. If you can't get proof against him then I'll try and frighten him off.'

'I wish I could think like you do,' Carter said.

Kelf swung his horse and rode to the Thompson house. He met Josie in the alley, on her way to do some shopping. She cried when he gave her the news about her father's men who had been killed. She had known most of them since her childhood. Kelf went on to the house to talk to John.

'It was my fault,' he told his brother. 'I should have been ready for a gun trap but it happened almost before we reached Stratton grass. When I go back it will be different, I promise you.'

'Don't take it personal, Brent,' John advised. 'Let it go for now and cool down.'

'That's the last thing I'll do,' Kelf said heavily. 'I want supplies for at least three days, and when I come back I'll have one or both of the Strattons hogtied.'

'When are you planning on riding out?'

'As soon as it's dark. I'll take a look around the

town now, and make a call at the doc's house. I'll
come back later.'

Kelf's thoughts were introspective as he walked
across the street to Doctor Farrell's house – dark,
hazy thoughts not rooted in reality. The doctor
answered his knock and nodded when he saw Kelf.

'I've been expecting you to call,' Farrell greeted.
'But then Thompson's wounded men showed up and
I got the whole sorry tale of what happened. And
some of your posse men ran from the fight. Do you
want to come in, or are you just passing? There's
blood on you in a couple of places so I'd better have
a look at you.'

'I need to talk to Sheriff Denton,' Kelf said. 'Is he
well enough?'

'You can see him.' Farrell grimaced. 'I think he's
playing a deep game. He's not as badly hurt as he
makes out. I've got a feeling that he doesn't want to
be seen, or talked to. He's acting like a man who's
swallowed something he can't digest. If you want to
move him to the jail you can do so.'

'I don't have the authority to do that. I'm not a
lawman.'

'Then you should be. I'm not involved in this situation. By the nature of my job I can stay outside it.
I'm the only qualified doctor for a hundred miles in
any direction.'

'You're a lucky man, Doc. Where will I find the
sheriff?'

'Go up the stairs. It's the third door on the left.'

103

Kelf entered the house and ascended the stairs. He opened the door of the last room on the left and peered inside to see Sheriff Denton lying in a bed, propped up so he could peer through the window at the street. His face was pale, his eyes showing signs of a fever. A small, thin man was seated beside the bed, and when Kelf walked into the room he got to his feet in a hurry and made for the door.

'There's no need for you to go, Ossie,' Denton said. 'This visitor won't be staying long.'

Kelf put out his left hand when Ossie tried to pass him. The little man halted like a nervous horse.

'Is your name Ossie Leavold?' Kelf asked.

'There's only one Ossie in this town,' Denton said, 'and his other name is Leavold.'

'I've got to get back to work,' Leavold said.

'I want to talk to you after I've spoken to the sheriff,' Kelf told him. 'Are you armed?'

'I never wear a gun. I'm not a fighting man.'

'Then where's the gun you threatened Lem Tolliver with a short time ago?'

Leavold seemed to shrink in stature. He opened his jacket and Kelf saw a pistol tucked into his waist-band. Kelf leaned forward, snaked out the gun, and held it in his hand. It was not pointing at Leavold but the little man squirmed as if he expected to be shot.

'Go back to your chair,' Kelf told him as if talking to a child. 'I'll get around to you in a minute.'

'What do you want with me?' Denton demanded.

'You were shot by one of Stratton's men out at my

104

brother's place. Does that mean Stratton wants to finish your relationship with him or were you shot by accident?'

'I never had anything to do with Stratton.' Denton's eyes narrowed and he groaned when he moved spasmodically in the bed and started pangs through his wounded shoulder. 'What the hell are you talking about, Kelf?'

'You know only too well, Sheriff. I don't have any details at the moment, but I expect to know all about your activities around here by the time I get through with the Strattons.'

Denton opened his mouth to protest but Kelf made a motion with the gun he was holding and the law man subsided.

'I don't want any lies, so don't talk. Just listen. When you're able to sit a horse, you'd better shake the dust of this place off your boots and hit the trail. If I ever set eyes on you again after this I'll call you out and kill you. Have you got that?'

'You can't tell me what to do,' Denton blustered.

'I'm not telling you anything. I'm just warning you, OK?' He moved closer to the bed, and suddenly the muzzle of the gun in his hand was pressing against Denton's forehead, right between the eyes. 'This is the only kind of language you and men like you understand. I won't repeat the advice, but you'll know I'm not fooling, so be long gone as soon as you're fit to travel.'

Denton remained motionless when Kelf removed

the gun from his forehead. Kelf turned to Leavold, who was rigid in fear.

'Let's you and me take a stroll along the street, Ossie. There are things about the set-up around here that maybe you can fill me in on. Come on, stir your hocks. I've got a lot to do today, so let's get to it.'

Kelf walked to the door and jerked it open. He looked back at Denton, who was watching him with an unblinking gaze. Leavold passed him and departed, almost falling down the stairs in his haste. They left the doctor's house and began to walk along Main Street.

'Let's go get a beer to show there's no ill feeling between us,' Kelf said.

'I don't wanta be seen around here in your company,' Leavold said sharply.

'So let's take a stroll down to the livery barn so we can talk. I want to know why you're a Stratton man and how far you'd go to do what Stratton tells you.'

'I'm not a Stratton man!' Leavold's eyes were bulging out of his head and he was quaking. Light-weight and small-boned, the top of his head barely reached Kelf's shoulder.

'It looks like everyone else is, so why should you be different? Let's just say that I believe you're working for the Strattons. You take orders from the sheriff, who was put into office by the Strattons. What was he telling you to do before I came into that bedroom? It could only be more trouble for men like my brother and Jeff Thompson, and I'm waging war against anyone who has designs on my brother's ranch and family.'

'I wouldn't do anything like that!' said Leavold in a trembling tone.

'What is Stratton really after around here? He's got the town under control, and most of the towns-folk obey him, even to the point of murder. What more could he want in town? He's after my brother's ranch, so is he making a play for more range?'

'Don't ask me. I don't know a thing. I don't have any property.'

'What's your job in town?'

'I ain't got a job at the moment.'

'So how do you live? I don't think the folks here are strong on charity.'

'I do odd jobs, anything that comes along.'

'Is that why you joined that raid on the freight depot?' Kelf was peering along the street. He saw Josie coming out of the general store carrying a pile of shopping, and stiffened when a man who was lounging against an awning post outside the store suddenly approached her and grasped her arm. He started running towards the store. Josie dropped her shopping, and the man began to force her into the alley beside the store.

Kelf ran through a group of townsfolk on the side-walk, scattering them. He could hear Josie screaming, and hurled himself into the alley beside the store. He cannoned into a wall and almost lost his balance. He saw Josie lying on the ground, kicking out at the man, who was trying to drag her up off the ground. Kelf kept moving. He was holding Ossie Leavold's pistol, and levelled it at the man, who had heard his approach and was turning to face him, reaching for his holstered gun.

Kelf triggered the gun and the thunder of the weapon threw a string of echoes across the town. The man jerked under the strike of the bullet, tripped over his own feet, and then sprawled on his face. Kelf halted beside Josie and bent down to help her up. The relief which came to her face when she saw him was overwhelming. She was breathless and shocked, and took hold of Kelf's shoulders and leaned her weight against him.

'My knees have turned weak,' she said, breathing deeply. She glanced at the motionless man and then averted her gaze, suppressing a shudder.

Kelf turned and examined the man and found he was dead. The bullet had struck him in the side of his neck, just under the ear.

'Do you know him?' he asked.

She studied the dead face for long moments, and then shook her head. 'I have seen him around town, but not very often. Will you take me home, Brent?'

He nodded and took her arm. He was still carrying his pistol. It was a natural extension to his hand. As they reached the alley mouth, Carter came hurrying along the sidewalk. He was sweating and breathless when he arrived.

'What happened?' he demanded.

Josie told him, and then went to collect her scattered shopping.

'It's a good thing you were around,' Carter observed. He walked into the alley and looked at the dead man. His face was grave when he came back to Kelf's side.

'He's Hank, one of the Jennis brothers,' he said. 'Cole is the other one. They're top guns for Stratton, and you've killed one of them. Now you'll have to do for the other, or he'll get you. Why was he after Mrs Kelf, do you reckon?'

'To put more pressure on my brother and Jeff Thompson, I guess.' Kelf stuck Ossie Leavold's gun in his waistband. 'I've told Sheriff Denton to get out of town the minute he's able to ride.'

'What did he say to that?'

'Not much. He obviously thinks the Strattons will protect him. He'll change his mind pretty damn quick when he has to face me in the street.'

'Don't go for him until he's been fired from his job. We could have a situation where I might have to come for you.' Carter's face was bleak.

'Who is the top man on the town council?'

'Frank Jex. He owns the general store.'

'Is he Stratton's man?'

'It's hard to say. If he isn't then why hasn't Stratton moved in on him?'

'I'll ask him.' Kelf laid a hand on Carter's sleeve as Josie came back to them carrying her shopping. 'Take Josie home, will you? I'll push this situation as far as I can now I've got my teeth into it.'

Carter nodded. 'And watch out for Cole Jennis. He and his brother are never far apart.'

Kelf turned to Josie. 'I've got something to do so go along with Mr Carter. He'll see you safely home.'

Josie opened her mouth to protest, but decided against it when she saw his expression. She nodded, and Carter held out a hand to relieve her of some items of her shopping. When they moved along the alley to the back lot, Kelf went into the store.

Several women were in the shop, shaken by the shooting outside. They stared at Kelf, and as if by a secret signal they departed like a gaggle of geese. The tall, thin man in a white apron behind the counter was standing with his hands palm downwards and his head bowed, as if lost in contemplation of some great problem. He looked at Kelf and heaved a sigh as he shook off his thoughts.

'It's a bad business when a woman can't come shopping without being confronted by a hard case,' Kelf said.

'Is he dead?' Frank Jex's lips barely moved.

'As a door nail! He pulled a gun on me. I'm Brent Kelf, John Kelf's brother. It was lucky for my sister-in-law that I was around, huh?'

Jex did not reply. Kelf eyed him for a moment, and then asked, 'Why are you dragging your heels over the problem of what to do about Sheriff Denton? You must know he's a Stratton man. Carter can't do a blamed thing until he's officially made

110

sheriff, and while you and your council do nothing the situation in this town gets worse. I don't understand you, Mr Jex, unless you're under the Stratton heel.'

'I am not!' Jex straightened and he glared at Kelf, became animated. 'I have to go along with my fellow councillors, and I have my doubts about some of them. But I won't dally longer. I'll see that the situation is restored, and I'll start right now. If you'll leave, I'll lock up and get about my business.'

Kelf went out to the street. Jex removed his apron and picked up a coat. He emerged from the store and locked the door.

'Thank you for reminding me of my civic duty,' he said, and strode off along the sidewalk.

Kelf returned to the Thompson house. When he walked in, he saw a badly shocked Josie, telling John about the incident outside the store.

'So you killed one of the Jennis brothers,' John said.

Brent nodded. 'One down and one to go,' he said.

'This is no joking matter.' John shook his head. 'The situation is getting worse and worse, and I'm wondering where it will end. It's an evil business when women are dragged into men's badness.'

'It won't last much longer,' Brent said. 'I'm riding out at sundown.'

'You should leave right now,' Josie said. 'As soon as Cole Jennis learns that you killed his brother, he will turn over the town to get at you.'

Kelf considered for a moment and then nodded. 'You're right. I'm only wasting time here. I'll need supplies for about four days.'

'I'll fill a sack with what you'll need,' said Josie immediately, 'and you'd better take a spare canteen in case you can't get water out on the range.'

She hurried into the kitchen and busied herself, relieved to have something to do. Kelf checked his gun and he was ready to leave.

'I'll take a walk along the street before I pull out,' he said.

'I'll put your supplies on your horse,' Josie told him.

He left the house and went to Main Street, where he paused and stood on the sidewalk, looking around. There were still some townsfolk standing in groups, expecting more trouble to start. He saw Carter standing at the door of the law office, and Frank Jex was with the lawman, waving his hands and talking fast. Carter was nodding, and Kelf hoped Jex was imparting some good news to the deputy.

Two riders were moving into the street from out of town. Kelf caught their movement and watched them rein up outside the saloon. He saw Ossie Leavold emerge from the saloon and engage the two new-comers in conversation. The little man had a lot to say, and pointed towards the spot where Kelf was standing. One of the riders jerked on his reins and came along the street at a lope.

Kelf loosened his pistol in its holster and flexed the fingers of his right hand. He knew what was coming and he was ready for it. . . .

EIGHT

The rider slowed and reined into the sidewalk just before he reached Kelf's position. He dismounted and trailed his reins before turning to face Kelf. Tall and grim-faced, he was dressed in dusty range clothes, a yellow bandana knotted around his neck. The cartridge belt buckled around his slim waist had a holster low on his right side, tied down to his thigh with a leather thong. He moved with grim deliberation, his eyes burning with an intentness and determination that pushed him into a situation which had only one conclusion.

'You're Brent Kelf!' It was a statement rather than a question.

Kelf nodded. 'Ossie Leavold told you who I am. I shot your brother earlier. He was molesting my sister-in-law, and pulled his gun when I went to help her.'

Jennis backed away from his horse towards the centre of the street, his right hand down at his side, fingertips brushing the butt of his gun.

114

'I'm gonna kill you, Kelf, and then I'll call out your brother and kill him. I came into town to do just that.'

Kelf stepped down into the dust of the street. In the background, men were scattering to get out of the line of fire. Jennis halted and waited stolidly. Kelf halted opposite him with a distance of some twenty feet between them, his concentration focused on the lone figure before him.

Time seemed to slow down, became non-existent. For endless moments there was no movement between them. Then Jennis eased the fingers of his right hand towards the butt of his pistol. His face took on a scowl.

'What are you waiting for?' He sneered. 'The only chance you've got is to draw first!'

'It's your call, your fight,' Kelf replied. 'All you've got to do is pull your hogleg clear of leather. I'm wondering what you're waiting for.'

Jennis cursed. His eyes were like coals poked into his face with a branding iron. His fingers darted like a striking snake to his holstered gun and he drew the weapon with all the skill and experience he could muster.

Kelf, filled with keen anticipation, slipped effort-lessly into his sequence of action as if Jennis's brain controlled them both. His pistol cleared leather. He was a split second faster than Jennis. His gun muzzle levelled and a shot cracked heavily. Jennis jerked, stopped his action before his muzzle cleared its holster. He reeled backward, hands lifting to his chest, where a splotch of blood had suddenly appeared. His life ran out of his body like water pouring from an up-ended canteen. He came loose at the neck, waist and knees, and dropped lifelessly to the ground. Echoes chased raucously across the street. . . .

The sound of pounding hoofs cut through Kelf's concentration and he turned to face the direction from which the sound came A pistol crashed and a string of echoes were tossed into the back trail of the shot that had killed Jennis. The rider who had entered town with the dead man was spurring his horse and coming fast at Kelf, waving his gun. He fired a second shot, and Kelf heard it crackle by his left ear.

Kelf clenched his teeth as he lifted his gun. The rider was barely twenty yards away and sighting his Colt for a third shot. Kelf triggered his pistol. The rider reeled sideways out of his saddle and fell heavily into the dust of the street. Kelf glanced around as he holstered his gun, and saw Carter running towards him along the boardwalk.

Carter was grinning, filled with a blend of excitement and relief. 'Say, I just got the go ahead from Frank Jex to take on the sheriff's job. I was coming to tell you when I saw Jennis moving in and you let him draw first! Heck, Kelf, he wasn't in your class, and him acting like he could beat anyone in the world. Will you join my posse? We work well together, and we could put an end to the trouble pronto if we play our cards right. I need to get after those rustlers in Rainbow Valley before they slip away, and I aim to round up the Strattons and close down their bad business.'

'Count me in,' said Kelf without hesitation. 'I was waiting for sundown, when I reckoned to head out and do the job on my lonesome, but a posse will get it done legally.'

'There are some men in town I know I can rely on, and I've sent them word to be ready at the livery barn in an hour. I want to call in on Andy Murdoch at his spread. He'll wanta be in on catching the rustlers. I'll see you at the stable, huh?' Carter was already moving away, but he paused and added, 'I've got a jailer coming in to run things in town until I get back, and Doc Farrell will let me know when Denton will be fit to occupy one of my cells. That ex-sheriff ain't gonna get away with anything. My guess is that folks will be rushing the jail to put the deadwood on him, the bad things he's done in the name of the law.'

'You look to be organized. But if you're going for the rustlers first – and I think you should – then I'll follow my original plan and make for the Stratton spread to pick up the top men.'

'That's OK by me, but the way you operate, most of the men you go for wind up dead.' Carter grinned. 'If you grab either of the Strattons, you'll come straight back to town with him, huh?'

117

Kelf nodded. 'I'm hoping to pick up both of them; and maybe I can bring 'em in alive.'

Carter departed, and Kelf heard him shouting orders to men along the street. It sounded as if the local law department had recovered from its bout of bad handling and was finally set to put matters right. He turned into an alley and returned to the Thompson house.

Josie had put his supplies in a sack and he took his leave and went to the freight stable for his horse. He preferred to work alone, accustomed as he was to bounty hunting, and when he rode out, he was encompassed by a feeling of relief. He headed in the opposite direction to the Stratton ranch until he was out of sight of the town, and then turned north, circling until he reached the trail where he had first met Josie. He continued through the mid-afternoon until he reached his brother's ranch, and a long sigh of bitterness filled him when he saw that the ranch house had been burned. A pile of smouldering wood marked the end of John's cattle business.

He went on indomitably, impatient now for the final showdown, following a well-beaten trail that went on past the ruins of the Big K ranch. Shadows were beginning to gather in the low places when he topped a rise and reined in to look at a large cattle ranch occupying the crest of a low ridge, below which a shimmering creek, fed by the uplands farther north, was hemmed in by the low hills surrounding it. A collection of barns and sheds were off to the left, with a couple of large corrals farther left. One corral contained at least a dozen horses; the other was seething with a herd of bawling steers.

There were no humans in sight, and he spent a long time watching the spread for signs of life. He saw no movement anywhere; no smoke coming from the cook shack chimney, which was situated close to the bunk house, and was significant because this part of the day was a ranch cook's busiest time, preparing the main meal for riders coming in after a hard day's work.

He circled the ranch until he reached the rear, found a gully where he could conceal his horse, and left the animal on a loose rein so it could graze unhindered. He ascended the ridge until he reached a spot just behind the larger of the two barns. The shadows were growing longer. The sun was on its downward path to the western horizon and the sky was losing it brassy quality, which was being replaced by a deeper blue that slowly changed into purple.

Silence lay over the ranch like a blanket. Kelf could hear the steady thump of the pulse in his right temple. He checked his pistol and then made for the bunk house. If the ranch was working normally he should find the crew there, waiting to eat. He reached the cook shack and paused to peer in through a window. A short fat man wearing a dingy apron was busy at a stove. Kelf moved on and peered through a rear window in the bunk house, and was surprised to find it empty. He went back to the cook shack and entered, his right hand close to his holstered gun.

The cook grinned at the sight of him. 'I'm glad to see you,' he greeted. 'The place has been dead since old man Stratton rode out with the crew. Who are you anyway? You're a stranger.'

'I've got a message for Adelaide,' Kelf bluffed. 'I was at Rainbow Valley yesterday when she rode in.'

'Well, you're in luck. She showed up here about two hours gone. She's over in the house. I went over a short time ago to ask if she wanted some grub, and it looked like she was packing to leave.'

'I thought she was not allowed to leave. That's what she said yesterday. She had a man guarding her so she couldn't light out. What's changed?'

'That's the way it goes around here. Do you want some grub? I've got enough ready for fifteen men and there's no one here to eat it. They could have told me what time they would be back and I would have known when to start preparing.'

Kelf shook his head. 'I'd better not stay now I know Adelaide is here. You know what she's like if she doesn't get everything her own way. I'll be seeing you.'

He departed into the gathering gloom. There was a lighted window now in the front of the ranch house, and he moved silently through the shadows, drawn like a moth to a flame. He stepped on to the porch. The light-stained window was on the ground floor. He tapped sharply on the door and it was opened almost immediately. Adelaide gazed at him open-mouthed for a couple of minutes and then smiled.

'I didn't think I'd see you again,' she said. 'Come on in and keep me company. This place is like a grave. Who have you come to see? Willard is still in Rainbow Valley. He wasn't well enough yesterday to make the trip to town. I was surprised when I got here to find my father had ridden out earlier with the entire crew to attend to a little problem that came up with one of the smaller ranchers.'

'That means trouble for someone,' Kelf commented, stepping into the house, and Adelaide smiled again.

'It's the only way to deal with hard-nosed men who will never back off an inch. You should know that because you have to shoot almost every man you run into, and you don't take any prisoners. I like the way you manage your life. I wish I could do the same. There are some men around here I'd like to shoot.'

'You wore a gun yesterday,' Kelf observed. 'And you weren't slow in using it.'

He looked around the big sitting room, which had obviously been furnished by a man, although there were feminine touches like chintz curtains at the two windows and a couple of vases filled with wild flowers. The big three-seat sofa was covered with brown leather, as were the matching easy chairs. A gun rack was nailed over the fire place containing two shot guns and a Winchester rifle. A cavalry sword with a citation occupied the centre of the back wall, and a colourful Indian blanket was fixed to a third wall with several other Indian relics around it.

'Sit down and get comfortable,' Adelaide invited. 'Would you like a drink?'

He declined. 'I don't drink while I'm working,' he told her, 'and I'm not here for pleasure.'

'Are you planning to shoot someone?' A smile played on her lips, but her eyes were unfathomable, with the sharp glint of alertness in their depths.

'That would be telling.' He smiled back. 'But it all depends on the reception I get from the male members of your family.'

'I know what the situation is between you and Willard – you'll shoot on sight after yesterday – and if it isn't Willard then it must be my father you're after. What has he done to attract your attention?'

'I came by my brother's ranch on my way here. It had been burned to the ground.' His face was expressionless but conveyed grim determination. 'I'm holding your father responsible. If he didn't do it personally then some of his men acted on his orders, and that's good enough for me. Who stole the steers in Rainbow Valley?'

'Why should that worry you?'

'I don't want to kill the wrong people. I suspect that the herd has been moved out of the valley since yesterday.'

'They were moved out last night. My father has a theory about those steers. He thinks someone stole them and ran them into Rainbow Valley so it would look as if he was responsible for the rustling. That's why Dad is not on the ranch right now. He's gone to take up the matter with the man he thinks is responsible.'

Kelf sat down. He was thinking about Carter and the posse, and what the deputy might do when he discovered the herd gone. He'd arrest Willard and send him back to town, and then he would come on here, ready for a showdown. He wondered if Adelaide was telling the truth. He'd discovered yesterday that she lied whenever it suited her.

The sound of hoofs approaching the house alerted Kelf and he drew his pistol before Adelaide was aware of the intrusion. He moved to stand by the door, gun ready for action. Adelaide reacted swiftly. She moved to his side and pushed down his gun until the muzzle was pointing at the floor.

'No shooting,' she warned in a low tone. 'Stand behind the door when I open it.'

Kelf nodded. A moment later, there was a knock at the door. Adelaide opened it a few inches and peered out. Kelf could see her profile. It was firm and expressionless. She certainly had her share of cold nerve.

'Hi, Ossie,' she said as a man greeted her in a low tone. 'What are you doing this far from town? Where's my father? Why isn't he home?'

'I came to warn him of what's been happening in town,' said Ossie Leavold. 'There's been hell to pay,

Miss Stratton. Sheriff Denton has been jailed. Carter is the sheriff now, and he left town with a posse which is heading for Rainbow Valley. That bounty hunter – Brent Kelf – killed both the Jennis brothers in town, and he left about the same time the posse did. Will you tell Mr Stratton I was here? I'd better be getting back to town to see what else has been going on.'

Kelf jerked the door fully open and Adelaide moved aside surprisingly quickly. He levelled his gun at Leavold and jabbed the muzzle into the little man's chest. Leavold uttered a cry of fear and turned to run. Kelf grabbed a handful of his shirt front, restrained him, and he sagged against Kelf's hand as if he had already been shot.

'Don't shoot me!' Leavold gasped.

'What have you done that would make me kill you?' Kelf demanded. 'You're a weasel, Ossie. Your tongue is so long you'll trip over it before this business is done. As you're so fond of gabbing about folks, tell me where the Stratton crew have gone, and what business they're at.'

'I heard yesterday that Andy Murdoch was gonna get hit because he's been making hostile noises about Mr Stratton.' Leavold's face was white as a sheet. He looked fearfully at Adelaide, hoping for some kind of back-up but she turned her back on him, her face expressing disgust.

'You knew that and didn't tell Carter?' Kelf tightened his grip on Leavold's shirt front and shook him until his teeth rattled. 'If anyone at Murdoch's place is killed, I'll see you'll hang for keeping your mouth shut about this. You're a sawn-off runt with no guts, and you don't deserve to live with decent folks. You'd talk about your own mother if you thought it would earn you a dollar!' He shook Leavold again, and when he released his hold on the shirt, the little man fell in a heap on the floor.

'Don't kill him in here,' Adelaide said. 'Pa would be angry if blood got spilled on the carpet. It came all the way from Sacramento.'

'Have you got a gun on you?' Brent bent and slapped Leavold's pockets, felt a hard object in one, and drew out a Derringer .41. He checked that the weapon was loaded and put it in his pocket.

'Were you planning on shooting someone?' Kelf resumed his hold on Leavold's shirt and lifted him to his feet.

'You'd better take him out of here before my father returns with the crew,' Adelaide suggested. 'You can't fight them all, and you'd better go to the Murdoch place and see what's happened. Murdoch is married and has a couple of kids.'

'It will be too late by now.' Kelf shook his head. 'Your crew left hours ago.'

'They weren't planning to go to Murdoch's place until they'd got the herd started out of Rainbow Valley,' she replied.

Kelf thrust Leavold towards the door. 'We're riding together, Ossie, and you'll show me where Murdoch lives. Don't even think of trying to get away from me or you'll hit the trail to hell faster than a horse can gallop. I'll see you again, Adelaide.'

'But not here,' she replied. 'I wouldn't want to be responsible for your death.'

Kelf departed with Leavold, and made the little man lead his horse to the rear of the ranch to the spot where Kelf's horse was waiting.

'Listen, Ossie,' Kelf said. 'Do one good thing in your life. Show me the way to Murdoch's place and I'll let you go.'

'I can't trust you.'

'As I see it, you don't have a choice. Just show me Murdoch's ranch and you can beat it and I won't bother you again.'

'Let's go,' Leavold said, and swung into his saddle.

'Don't try to slip away from me in the dark,' Kelf cautioned him. 'If you do escape, I'll track you down and kill you.'

'You're wasting time. Let's ride.'

Kelf dropped back a couple of yards and followed Leavold's dim figure as they rode through the shadowy night. There was no moon, although the sky was aglitter with the sparkle of countless stars. Leavold did not falter, and rode steadily until, two hours later, he reined in.

'We're there,' he said.

'Where's the spread? I can't see a damn thing.'

'You're on the trail which leads into Murdoch's front yard. All you've got to do is let your horse follow it.'

'No dice! I don't trust you, Ossie. Take me within sight of the ranch house and then you're free to go.'

Leavold cursed under his breath and went forward again, eventually halting in deep shadow. Kelf looked around. He caught a glimpse of the roof of a small house, and saw part of a fence. The place was in darkness, and heavy silence pressed down in the night.

'Ride with me to the house. You'll be free to leave as soon as I hear Murdoch's voice.'

'Jeez, are you afraid of the dark?' Leavold kicked his horse forward. 'You better sing out before we get across the yard or you might get a bullet through your hat. It ain't safe to ride into a spread after dark, what with the trouble that's been going on.'

'We'll take that chance,' Kelf replied. 'Just be ready to duck if slugs start flying.'

The night was impenetrable. The breeze was cool but Kelf was sweating. It was a good sign that silence reigned hereabouts. Their hoofs sounded on the hard ground of the yard. Leavold began to drop back. Then the silence was broken by a hard voice calling from the inky blackness surrounding the house.

'Hold and declare yourselves. Get your hands up until we can check on you.'

'I'm Brent Kelf. We met at my brother's ranch. I've come to warn you that Stratton's crew left their spread earlier with the intention of paying you an unfriendly visit.'

'We're on our guard, and we're ready to fight. Do

you want to come in and talk?'

'I've come to stay, if you need me, and I'll stand with you against Stratton.'

'Who is that with you?'

'He's just a man who offered to show me the way here. He'll be riding out now.'

'Come on in, Kelf. I've got four men with me so I ain't too worried about anyone riding in on the prod.'

'Get the hell out of here, Ossie,' Kelf said. 'And if you've got any sense, you'll ensure that our paths don't cross again.'

Leavold vanished instantly. Kelf rode on towards the house, and as he reached the porch, the night was split asunder by a shattering volley of gun fire. The darkness was shredded by reddish muzzle flame and the silence was swept away by the sound of hammering guns. Kelf vacated his saddle in a low dive, hit the ground with a stunning impact, and was pinned down by the long outburst of crackling slugs that swept across the dark yard.

NINE

The shooting was coming from each side of the yard, and about twelve guns were shooting. Kelf kept his head down and began to slither into the shadows surrounding the porch. He was dimly aware of his horse running to the right and turning in behind the house, and when he reached the porch he crawled beneath it and went towards the far end, where he emerged beside the house. The shooting continued without a break, and furious echoes were being flung across the range.

Kelf watched the shooting. It was all directed at the house, and several flashing guns were replying to the onslaught from inside. Kelf moved to his left, saw where a line of five guns were throwing lead at the house, and set out to circle around them and take the action to them. He crawled under the fence and eased out several yards to get behind the position of the gun men, and then began to stalk the nearest in the line.

The nearest gunman was lying in cover at the line of the fence, easing up to observe and fire a shot and then dropping down again. Kelf heard several bullets coming from the ranch house crackle over his head, and he kept low. He moved only when the gunman raised to fire a shot, and approached carefully, getting almost to an arm's length before the man detected his presence. Kelf lunged forward when the gunman turned his head and saw him, his pistol already lifting to deliver a blow. The man tried to duck away but Kelf swung his gun and it thudded heavily against the man's head. He collapsed without a sound.

Kelf picked up the man's gun and hurled it into the surrounding darkness. He did not pause but set out to attack the next man, and dealt with him in a similar manner, disarming him and leaving without means of attack. But the third man he approached must have suspected something was amiss because the guns on his right had stopped shooting. He saw Kelf, who was still out of reach, and swung to aim his pistol in Kelf's direction. Kelf triggered his gun and the man flopped onto his face.

'There's shooting coming from my right,' a man shouted, and started shooting in Kelf's direction. Kelf flattened out, his gun ready, and drove a bullet into the man when he got up to move to a different position.

Two more gunmen turned their attention to Kelf, and he became involved in a private war that continued until one of the bad men was hit. The other moved back and the shooting ceased. Kelf looked around. The attack had lost its intensity. There were two gaps in the line firing from the opposite side of the yard. The shooting became desultory. Kelf thought it was time to get into the house. He crawled back the way he had come, checking for the men he had knocked out of the fight. They had gone, but they were unarmed and of no consequence.

The shooting died away until full silence reigned. Echoes faded into nothing. Kelf listened intently to the night noises. Wildlife had been disturbed by the shooting. A horse had caught a stray bullet somewhere out in the darkness and was protesting shrilly. Kelf suddenly picked up the distant sound of pounding hoofs and reloaded his gun. He waited motionless for developments, still at the top of his alertness.

'Hello, the house,' a voice called. 'This is Sheriff Carter with a posse. What's going on here?'

'I'm glad you've showed here,' Andy Murdoch replied. 'We've just beaten off an attack by about a dozen men. Brent Kelf is out there somewhere.'

'I'm over here,' Kelf shouted. He climbed over the fence and approached the house as the posse came into the yard through the gate.

A lamp was lighted in the house and Andy Murdoch emerged to stand on the porch. He hung the lantern on a hook over his head. He was holding a pistol in his right hand. Carter dismounted beside Kelf. His teeth gleamed when he smiled.

'We didn't have any luck at Rainbow Valley,' he said. 'The herd had been moved out. I left a couple of men there to follow tracks when it gets light. It looks like you got the best of the action. We heard a helluva fight going on here while we were still in the distance.'

'They didn't get close enough to give us much trouble,' Murdoch said. He glanced at Kelf. 'There were five guns firing from the left of the yard, and they cut off pretty damn quick. I guessed you had got in among them. Thanks for your help.'

'No trouble. I disarmed three of them, and they pulled out when they regained their senses. We need to look around here and see who was doing the shooting. We have to pick up Abe Stratton to put an end to the trouble.'

'We found Willard Stratton in the shack in Rainbow Valley,' Carter said. 'You put a slug through him. There were several of the AS crew with him, but they didn't put up much of a fight. I'm taking Willard back to town. He'll spend a long, long time in jail.' Carter studied Kelf's face. 'I guess you'll go for Abel Stratton, huh?'

'I won't give up.' Kelf shook his head. 'The trouble seems to be over here so I'll head back to the Stratton house and see what I can turn up.'

'We'll make a clean sweep through the town and run out all the men who backed the Strattons.' Carter was happy with the situation and his voice rang with satisfaction. 'When the range has been cleansed of rustlers we'll get the rustled stock back.'

Kelf began to withdraw. He was concerned about the situation. He knew Abel Stratton had left the AS with most of his crew, but had cut away from them somewhere on the range and now was probably raising hell somewhere.

'I have someone who knows where the rustled stock is being moved to,' Kelf said. 'I'll talk to her again, and let you know what I learn.'

He found his horse at the back of the ranch house and rode out, heading back to the Stratton place. He had a powerful sense of direction and moved steadily through the night. Tiredness was pulling at his mind and he dozed in the saddle, slipping out of and back into high alertness. When he saw the ranch it looked derelict, unoccupied – no lights anywhere, and he realized he would not be able to move in silently. He left his horse where it could not be discovered accidently, checked his pistol, and refilled the empty loops on his gun belt with fresh shells from his saddle bag before moving in to check for a guard.

He stood downwind of several small buildings, checking for the smell of cigarette smoke, and while he waited a sense of hostility flared in his mind. When he moved on, his alertness was at double strength and he carried his gun in his right hand. It was not until he was at the cook shack that he caught the tang of cigarette smoke. The shack was in darkness but when he moved closer to a window, he saw dim light issuing from within through the sacking that was suspended across the aperture. He moved to the door, cocked his gun and grasped the door handle. Thrusting the door open, he stepped into the shack.

A man was seated at a table with a mug of coffee before him, and he was completely surprised by Kelf's sudden appearance. Kelf closed the door swiftly and advanced on the man, who did not move, his face showing shock and disbelief. Kelf recognized him as one of the men he had seen in Rainbow Valley when he was there. The man made a tentative move to reach for his pistol, which was lying on the table, and Kelf spoke quickly.

'That would be a wrong move, mister. Put your hands up and sit still.'

The man obeyed, and Kelf moved in to take the gun. He pressed the muzzle against the right side of the man's neck.

'What's your name?' Kelf asked.

'Mike Newman.'

'Who's on the ranch?'

'Four of the crew – Miss Adelaide's in the house.'

'Where's Abel Stratton?'

'The hell if I know. I heard he'd left the ranch with the rest of the riders, and some of them turned up in the valley, but a posse from town rode in and Willard Stratton was arrested. I didn't see Abel at all. One of the crew mentioned that when they left here, Abel rode off alone, and looked to be heading for town.'

'What were you doing in the valley? I heard that

the steers had been moved out.'

'We were watching for pursuit to come from town.'

'Where are the rustled steers now?'

'You don't expect me to tell you that, huh?'

Kelf helped himself to a mug of coffee, his gun aimed at Newman's back.

'Let's go take a look at the rest of the crew. Are they in the bunk house?'

'One is in the house, making sure Adelaide doesn't get any ideas about sneaking off. The others are getting some sack-time. Everyone has been working darned hard lately.'

'What's the name of the man guarding Adelaide?'

'Tom Heffle.'

'So let's go rouse out the others. Bring that lamp so we don't walk in on them in the dark. I don't want to kill anyone I don't have to.'

Newman picked up the lamp and carried it when they moved out. He entered the bunk house ahead of Kelf and placed the lamp on a table. Three bunks were occupied by sleeping men.

'Come on, wake up.' Kelf shouted, and had to repeat the order twice before there was a reaction. One of the men opened his eyes, stared at the lamp, and demanded, 'Where's the fire?'

'There'll be gun fire if you don't get the hell out of that bunk and stick your hands up pronto.' Kelf grasped the foot of one of the other men and shook it violently. 'Come on, rattle your hocks.'

The three men arose, saw the gun in Kelf's hand

and stood motionless under its threat.

Kelf spoke to Newman. 'Get that lariat off the wall over there and tie these three. Do a good job. I'll check the knots.'

He watched intently until the men were hogtied on their bunks. He checked the knots and was satisfied they could not escape. Newman got on a bunk and Kelf roped him securely.

'You can go back to sleep now,' he told the men, 'and sleep as long as you like.'

He doused the light and left. As he walked to the ranch house he used his ears, listening for unnatural noises. The spread was like a graveyard, no movement; silent and still. He held his gun ready, paused when he reached the porch, and then stepped firmly on the boards. He put away his gun.

'Hey, Heffle,' he called. 'Where are you? Light a lamp. I don't want to get shot walking in on you. Newman told me you were here. I've got a message for Adelaide that won't wait until sunup.'

Silence followed his words but he was patient, and repeated what he had said. A few moments later, he saw a glimmer of light inside the house which flared into bright lamp light. Then a voice called, 'Who in hell is out there this time of the night? And who are you? I don't recognize your voice.'

'I've come from town. Abe Stratton told me to fetch Adelaide to him. Rouse her out of bed and tell her to get ready to ride with me.'

The door was opened. A bearded face peered out

136

at Kelf and a pistol was pointed at him.

'I ain't seen you around town.'

'I know your name. Newman told me to rouse you out. If you're not happy with my face then go check with Newman. He wasn't pleased to be roused at this time. And I ain't happy myself, being turned out like this.'

'Who the hell are you then? What's your name, and what do you do around town?'

'I'm Sheriff Denton's nephew. I've come down from Kansas to visit him, and found he'd been shot. Do you want my family history? I'll tell you some other time. The sooner I get back to town the sooner I can hit the sack, so cut out the questions and get moving.'

'You'd better come in and wait. Adelaide won't get ready inside of an hour, unless I miss my guess. What's the boss doing in town?'

'You can ask him the next time you see him.'

Kelf stepped into the house. Heffle was turning to fetch Adelaide, but flickering light was descending the stairs, and Adelaide's voice came floating down from above.

'What in tarnation is going on down here? Is that you, Pa?'

'It's a man come from town to take you there, Miss Adelaide,' Heffle said. 'He says he's the sheriff's nephew.'

Adelaide appeared at the foot of the stairs; holding a small lamp. She was wearing a cloak over her nightdress, and looked as if she had been disturbed from a sound sleep. When she recognized Kelf, her expression changed.

'You fool, Heffle,' she said furiously. 'This man isn't the sheriff's nephew. He's John Kelf's brother, and he's the one been causing all the trouble we've been getting the last few days.'

Kelf saw Heffle's right elbow bend as the man reached for the butt of his pistol. He jerked his gun from its holster and covered Heffle before the man could make his play. Heffle blinked at the exhibition of such fast gun play and lifted his gun hand away from his pistol as if it had suddenly become too hot to handle.

'Get your hands up,' Kelf snapped. He moved in and took Heffle's pistol – searched him for other weapons and found none. 'Sit down over in that corner and don't move a muscle.'

Heffle scurried across the room and sat down in an old leather chair. Kelf eyed Adelaide through half closed eyes.

'I never know where I am with you,' he complained. 'You've done your best on our previous meetings to keep me out of your family's hands, and you wanted me to get you away from here. Now I've got the time to help you, you've changed your attitude and you're acting like the only thing that matters is having me shot by your crew. So what gives? Do you want to get away from your family or are you gonna stay here like a good girl? Just tell me so I know what to do. I haven't had much sleep the last couple of days, and I need to rest up for the next fight that will be coming up to finish this trouble.'

'I wanted the cattle returned to their rightful owners,' she replied, 'and that is going to happen. But I don't want my family killed. I can see clearly the kind of man you are. You won't stop until you're the last man standing. I agree that you're in the right, and I'm amazed at what you've done. But that's as far as I want you to go.'

'That's too bad. I have a family, and I'll go through hell and high water to protect them. The Strattons – father and son – are responsible for what's been going on around here, and there's only me to stop them. They are guilty men, and will have to face up to what they've done. So what do you want to do? Shall I take you to town and see you off to where you want to go?'

She shook her head. 'I don't know what to do,' she admitted. 'If I let you have your head my father and brother will be dead by tomorrow, and I'll have to spend the rest of my life suffering for letting you do what you have to.'

'That's your choice, and nobody can help you to make a decision.' Kelf shook his head. 'I wouldn't want to face that, and you have to decide now because I need to get moving.'

The anguish of Adelaide's situation showed clearly in her face, and Kelf felt a wayward pang of sympathy for her. She sat down on the bottom stair and put the lamp she was holding on the floor at her side. Kelf stifled a strand of impatience flitting through his mind, but he could see no way out for her. He was set on his intention to stop the Strattons, and was as unstoppable as a runaway train on the edge of a precipice.

He glanced at Heffle, and in the split second before he returned his gaze to Adelaide, she reached a decision. She snatched a pistol out of her dressing gown pocket; a small calibre hide-out gun, and fired a shot at Kelf.

The crash of the weapon filled the silent house with echoing thunder. Kelf felt a shaft of pain in his chest. An invisible hand thrust at him and he fell instantly into a black, bottomless pit that was filled with a roaring sound. His sight faded. Pinpoints of light flashed around him like shooting stars as he sagged into unconsciousness. . . .

Coming back to his senses was like fighting his way out of a black shroud, indistinct but nightmarishly real. His ears were filled with a roaring sound that hammered overloud until he emerged from the shock gripping him. He was aware of grinding pain somewhere in his chest. His eyes were closed and he did not seem able to open them. He heard sounds around him but could not identify them until he realized they were voices, and then they became clear, and he knew Adelaide was talking loud and fast against the protests of harsh male voices.

'You will not take him out and shoot him,' she said fiercely.

'Why the hell not?' someone replied. 'You just shot him.'

'Not to kill him. I don't want him dead,' Adelaide insisted. 'I want him out of action for a few hours. I must be tired, I guess, because I missed my mark and hit him harder than I meant to. Now get out of here before I give you all your marching orders.'

Kelf opened his eyes slowly. He saw Adelaide standing by the door to the front yard, and three of the remaining crew were bunched in the doorway. He recognized Newman and called to him.

'How did you get loose in the bunk house?'

Newman laughed. 'You forgot about the cook. He was in his room on the end of the cook shack, and waited until you came across here to the house before turning us loose. We came in as Adelaide shot you. Now she won't let us finish the job.'

'I told you to get out of here,' Adelaide cut in, her voice laced with impatience.

'We'll leave Heffle with you,' Newman said. 'Kelf is one big dangerous man.'

Adelaide got her way. The three cowhands departed. Kelf saw that Adelaide had her gun in her hand, and she came to stand over him – he was stretched out on the couch. There was a bowl of bloodied water beside the couch, and Kelf could feel that he had been bandaged. He looked around for Heffle, and saw the man sitting on a chair by the

141

door, a pistol in his hand.

'You're such a dangerous man I couldn't take any chances with you,' Adelaide told him, 'and I nearly killed you.'

'What kind of a crazy woman are you?' Kelf demanded. 'I bent over backwards to help you get clear of this range and you thank me with a bullet in the chest.'

'Just shut up and go to sleep,' she advised. 'You'll feel a lot better in the morning.'

He felt exhausted, and knew he didn't have the strength to get up and do what he knew must be done. It was as if his determination had seeped out of the bullet hole she had given him. He tried to keep his eyes open and his mind clear but found it impossible to fight the battle to remain alert. His eyes closed and a wave of listlessness began to steal through him. Adelaide must have thought that he had lost his senses again because she spoke harshly to the silent Heffle.

'Get moving now. Hitch up the buggy and put him in it. I'll take him into town to my father. Blood is thicker than water, after all.'

The words cut through the shock and inertia gripping him and he made an effort to overcome his condition. He opened his eyes, although it seemed to take all the effort he possessed. He looked from under lowered eyelids and watched Heffle get up and leave the house. Adelaide picked up her lamp and ascended the stairs. Kelf pushed himself to his feet. The pain of his action was overpowering until he stood erect and steadied his balance. He picked up his gun from a corner of the couch, checked it instinctively, reloaded a couple of empty chambers, and returned it to his holster. The weight of it on his hip was reassuring. He pressed his right hand against the left side of his chest and felt the stiffness of thick bandages.

He lounged on the couch, feet on the floor and his head against a big cushion, trying to coax the residue of his strength to gather and keep him going. Adelaide returned with a case. Time seemed to have no meaning – but it passed relentlessly. Heffle came back.

'The buggy is ready,' he reported tersely.

'Help me get him into it. It's time I was on my way,' Adelaide replied.

Between them, Adelaide and Heffle got Kelf out of the house and ensconced in a corner of the seat in the buggy. They did not notice the gun in his holster, and Kelf settled his mind to the inevitability of the situation. His only desire was to confront Abel Stratton, and they were taking him to do just that, and he was satisfied. . . .

TEN

Kelf slept on the way to town, his body steadily recouping his scattered senses and lessening his shock. When they reached Temple Rock, the time was close to midnight. He heard the sound of men's voices, and feigned unconsciousness when he was picked up and conveyed into a building. He heard Adelaide's voice throwing out orders, which were apparently obeyed without question, and he was finally laid on a bed and the commotion around him eased.

He wondered where he was but had no idea. Heffle was seated in a corner of the room, gun in hand, and appeared to be vigilant. Kelf considered the situation, and came to the conclusion that he would have to take advantage of any laxness on the part of his guard. When he tried to change his position to ease his wound he changed his mind and called Heffle.

'Give me a hand,' he said. 'My chest is hurting

something bad, and I can't change my position. Lift me up and turn me to the right, will you?'

'Stay where you are,' Heffle replied. 'I ain't coming within an arm's length of you. You're slicker than a wagonload of monkeys.'

Kelf felt for the butt of his gun, and clenched his teeth when he discovered it was no longer in his possession. He settled back to await Adelaide's return, dozing intermittently, and much later Adelaide entered the room. Her expression was morose, her eyes filled with worry.

'How are you feeling now?' she asled.

'Probably as bad as you're looking,' he replied. 'Have you found your father yet?'

'He rode out with a party of men some time before we arrived. Nobody seems to know where he's gone.'

'He's up to some devilment, I reckon. What place is this?'

'It's the freighter's house. It's been taken over as a headquarters.'

'What's happened to Jeff Thompson and my brother and his family?'

'They are being held as hostages to keep the townsfolk under control. Now don't start on me about it. I don't know anything. You'll have to talk to my father when he returns.'

'Are my brother and his family still in this house?'

'I don't know.' She did not meet his gaze.

'Well, you'd better find out where they are.'

She left the room without answering, and Kelf

made an effort to get to his feet.

'Where do you think you're going?' Heffle demanded. 'If you don't keep still on that couch, I'll put another slug through your ribs.'

Kelf eased his position. When the door opened again, he was surprised to see Ossie Leavold in the doorway.

'So you've come to the end of your trail, huh?' Ossie said. 'They're talking it over to pick the man who's gonna finish you off. They're all scared of you, and for them, the sooner you're dead and buried the better.'

'Get the hell out of here,' Heffle called. 'Leave the prisoner alone.'

'Who the hell do you think you're talking to?' said Ossie truculently. 'I work for the Strattons just like you, so where do you get off ordering me about?' He came into the room and closed the door, his expression ugly.

Kelf could see that Ossie was worked up as the little man confronted Heffle, who was grinning.

'Are you gonna call me out, Ossie?' he said. 'Heck, you ain't got the guts to take candy from a baby. Beat it before I swat you.'

Ossie walked to the window and peered out. When he turned around to depart, he had a gun in his right hand, and caught Heffle cold. The gunman was covering Kelf, and he looked sideways at Ossie, saw a pistol covering him and promptly opened his hand and dropped his gun to the floor. Ossie moved in, stepped behind Heffle, and slammed the barrel of his gun against the man's head.

'Come on, Kelf, get up and move out of here,' Ossie said in a tremoring tone. 'I'm being paid two hundred dollars to spring you out of here, and I'm keen to earn the dough.'

As Kelf struggled to his feet, Ossie picked up Heffle's gun and handed it to him.

'How many of Stratton's men are in the house?' Kelf asked.

'There are too many for you to handle in your condition. Get out of this window and head for the law office. There'll be big trouble around here when Abel Stratton gets back.'

'Who's gonna pay you for getting me out of here?'

'Jeff Thompson. He reckons you're the only man who can handle this bad deal.'

'Do you know where he and my family are being held prisoner?'

'Yeah, they're in the hotel with three guards watching them. You need to get them out of there pronto.' Ossie turned to the window and opened it. Kelf slipped the pistol into his holster and approached the window.

'It's lucky this room is on the ground floor,' he commented.

He sat on the window sill and put one leg over it. The pain in his chest flared to intolerable agony. Ossie thrust his hands against Kelf's back and pushed him out of the window. Kelf hit the ground heavily.

His senses begin to recede. He pushed to his hands and knees but could move no further. Ossie jumped through the window, regained his feet, and grasped Kelf's right arm. He lifted Kelf to his feet, ignoring Kelf's protests, and supported him as they moved away from the house.

'Run to the law office and get Carter to come here,' Kelf said. 'Tell him the situation. I can't go any further.'

'I won't do that. This is as far as I go,' Ossie turned away. 'I've earned my money. You're free and you're on your feet. Now it's up to you.' He left Kelf's side and disappeared into an alley.

Kelf entered the alley and leaned against a wall, pressing his hand against his right side. His senses receded and he struggled against falling into the black hole that seemingly appeared at his feet. He lurched forward and forced his legs into movement, not knowing what to do next but aware that he should be doing something. Thoughts of his brother raised urgency in his mind, and he entered Main Street and staggered towards the hotel.

He glanced into the lobby, fully expecting to see armed men waiting around, but there was no one in the reception area or at the desk. He entered and went to the office behind the desk, where a young woman was seated at a desk, working on figures in a ledger. She looked up at him when he called. She was in her middle twenties, fair-haired and blue eyed. She smiled at him and got to her feet.

'I'm sorry,' she said. 'Did you ring the bell on the reception desk? I didn't hear it. I'm Sue Hanson. My father owns the hotel. Do you require a room?'

'I'm Brent Kelf. My brother is John Kelf – Big K ranch. I was told he and his family were moved into the hotel. I'd like to see them.'

Her smile of welcome faded and she caught her breath. 'You've been hurt,' she gasped. 'There's blood on your shirt.'

'I'm not hurt bad. What about my family? Are they here?'

'They are in the hotel,' she replied, 'but I would advise you to stay away. They were brought in by Abel Stratton as hostages to draw you into the open, and he left three gunmen with them. It would be better if you went to see Sheriff Carter and talked to him about what can be done about the situation. If you tried to do anything on your own, there would be shooting, and your brother and his family could get hurt or possibly killed.'

He shook his head. 'There's no time to talk. If you went up to where they are being held, with some extra blankets or towels, and I followed you into the room when they let you in, I could get the drop on the gunmen and there wouldn't be any trouble.'

'I wouldn't try that.' She shook her head firmly. 'Josie Kelf is my friend, and the baby is with her. I'd never forgive myself if anything happened to them because of something I did.'

'It was just a thought, but maybe you're right. You

could go to the room, knock and ask them if there is anything they want, and I'll enter the room when they open the door.'

She shook her head. 'You don't look well enough to do anything. In your condition you'd surely make a mistake and it would all go wrong.'

'Where are the rooms they are in?'

'We put them in the big suite at the top of the house because they are your brother and his wife and child, and Mr Thompson, the freighter, who has been wounded. Three men are guarding them. They occupy a large double room and two smaller ones, all with connecting doors.'

'I'll go up there and take a look around.' Kelf lifted a hand when she started to protest again. 'If I don't do something they'll surely be killed when Able Stratton gets back to town. If you want to help then why don't you go for Sheriff Carter and ask him to bring some men here?'

She shook her head again, her mouth just a thin line.

'Then you'd better stay out of the way,' he responded grimly. 'I'm going up to settle this.'

'If you're set on going up there then I'll accompany you,' she spoke in a clipped tone, 'but I wish you would fetch the law yourself, and take precautions against your family getting hurt.'

'That's exactly what I'm going to do. It's all I've been doing since I came to Texas.' Kelf drew his pistol and checked the chambers.

He went into the lobby and headed for the stairs. Sue Hanson followed him, and they ascended the stairs silently. The hotel seemed strangely quiet, as if the guests had been moved out. When they reached the top floor, Kelf heard the sound of a child crying fretfully, and guessed it was his nephew.

He approached the nearest door, and Sue Hanson grasped his right arm and shook her head when he looked questioningly at her. She produced a key. Her face was pale but she looked resolute, and pointed to a door further along the corridor. Kelf nodded and took the key from her.

'You'd better go downstairs out of the way,' he advised.

She ignored his words and remained where she was. Kelf went to the door she had pointed out and tried it. To his surprise it opened to his touch. He paused, holding the door handle with his left hand. He cocked his pistol, and then pushed open the door and stepped into the room. It was empty.

He closed the door at his back. He could hear noises coming from the next room – Josie's voice raised in protest; a harsh male voice answering her, filled with threat and impatience. John spoke tensely, telling the man not to speak to his wife like that, and the man replied with a threat of violence. Kelf moved across the room, gauging the opposition against him. There were three gunmen, and they would not be close to one another to present him with an easy target.

He opened the door silently, tensed for action, and threw the door open wide and stepped quickly into the room, moved quickly to one side and lifted his gun as he looked around. John and Josie were seated on a couch in the big room, and the baby was in Josie's arms. Two men were seated at a table in a corner, playing cards. A third man was sitting in a big chair near the door to the corridor, reading a newspaper. Kelf breathed a swift prayer of relief.

He fired a shot into the ceiling and thunder filled the room. He saw the man with the newspaper jump out of his chair, dropping the newspaper and instinctively reaching for his holstered gun. Kelf snapped a shot at him, saw him fall, and turned his attention to the two men playing cards. One was frozen in shock; the other leaping up, overturning the table in his haste. Kelf waited until the man straightened to face him and then shot him in the centre of the chest. The room rocked to the explosions, and gun smoke tainted the air. The third man was slow getting into action. Kelf was covering him with his gun when he started his hand to his weapon.

'Have you got a death wish?' Kelf demanded. 'Don't touch that gun.'

The man lifted his hands, and Kelf crossed to him and took his pistol.

Kelf looked at the man who had been reading the newspaper. He was flat on his face and unmoving. The resistance was over. Josie was sitting very still, hugging her son, her hands over his ears, and a smile of relief came to her face when she recognized him. John's face broke into a grin. In the background, gun echoes were fading slowly. The split second of deadly action had reversed the situation. Kelf reloaded his gun and gave his brother a gun belt and a pistol from one of the dead men before moving to the door and opening it to call in Sue Hanson.

'What's going on?' Kelf asked the prisoner. 'Where's Abel Stratton?'

'I don't know. You'll see him soon enough, I guess.'

'I'll take you along to the jail,' Kelf said. He glanced at John.

'Keep the family together in here with the doors locked until I get back, John.'

John nodded and checked the gun. 'We'll be OK now,' he said grimly.

Kelf took his prisoner out of the hotel and they walked to the jail. Music and loud voices sounded in the big saloon. The law office was in silence, yellow light showing at the front windows. Under the menace of Kelf's gun, the prisoner opened the door and entered the office. Sheriff Carter was seated at his desk. A jailer sat at a corner of the desk, cleaning a rifle. Carter looked up when the door opened, and a grin came to his face when he saw Kelf. He got to his feet.

'I've been wondering how you were getting on,' he said. 'How have you been doing?'

'Didn't you hear the shooting?' Kelf said.

Carter shook his head. 'Anything north of the big saloon can't be heard here if the wind is in a certain direction.'

Kelf explained his experiences and Carter grasped the prisoner's arm and pushed him towards the desk.

'Lock up this one with the others, Mack,' he said to the jailer, and the man picked up a bunch of keys from the desk, drew his pistol, and herded the prisoner into the cells. 'The cells are nearly filled to overflowing,' Carter remarked. 'I've arrested a number of townsmen because they've been too friendly with the Strattons in the past. It's all I can do until Abel Stratton shows up. He's been busy on the range. Ben Wilson rode in earlier, and reported that his spread was attacked by masked riders. His two men were shot dead, and he was plugged in the back as he escaped.'

'Have you any idea where Stratton is now?' Kelf asked.

'If I knew I'd arrest him,' Carter said. 'I've got his son Willard in a cell, and he ain't going anywhere. You shot him pretty bad, and he's out of it now. I've got a few men on duty as special deputies, and I expect to get word of Abel Stratton's whereabouts the minute he shows his face in town.'

'Where does he stay when he's in town?'

'There's a house along Main Street, close to the general store, where he spends his free time. I reckon he's keen on Mary Turner, who owns the place.'

'Is it being watched?'

'Someone is keeping an eye on the area, and there's another man watching the saloon for men coming in from out of town. That's about all I can do. Now it's time to wait for word that he's back.'

'It's not enough for me,' Kelf said grimly. 'Show me Mary Turner's house and I'll watch it personally.'

Carter got his feet and walked to the door. 'Take care of the place until I get back, Mack,' he told the jailer. 'I'll be back soon.'

Kelf walked along the street with the sheriff, who paused in the alley beside the general store. The town was quiet except for the noise coming from the saloon. No one was on the street.

'That's Mary Turner's house, with the tree in the front garden,' Carter said. 'Watch it if you must, but don't raise a ruckus around town right now because it will only start my posse men into action, and be careful. They are all tense, and their trigger fingers are set to start shooting at the smallest thing.'

Kelf watched the sheriff walk back to the law office. He remained in the shadows of the store and waited, listening intently for unnatural sound. The wound in the side of his chest was throbbing painfully, and he lifted his left arm until he could press his elbow against the sore spot. Tiredness tugged at him. Hunger was like a rat gnawing in his stomach. He was thirsty, but fought down the desire to visit the saloon.

He had a feeling that the climax of the trouble was

due. Abel Stratton had been away from town all day, and he had been busy. It was a near certainty that he would return soon, and Kelf was ready and waiting for him.

He walked along the length of the alley to the back lots, and stood in stringent darkness. He leaned against the wall of the store, and had to use all of his determination to remain on his feet.

The click of a horse shoe striking a rock somewhere in the vast expanse of night caught his attention and he drew his gun, his discomfort swilling out of him as he came to full alertness. The sound was repeated, and he cocked his pistol. It was too dark to see anything, but he heard enough to accept that more than one horse was being led across the back lots. He heard the creak of saddle leather, the laboured breathing of horses, and then a harsh voice spoke in a penetrating tone.

'Some of you go along to the front of the jail and start shooting; the rest of you get around the back here. Pile on the pressure. I want Willard out of that jail pronto. Anyone who kills Carter will get ten dollars. Get moving now, and when we've finished with the jail, we'll start on the town and get it back under our control.'

Kelf didn't want Stratton's men to deploy. He lifted his gun, aiming in the general direction of the rancher's voice.

'Stratton, you and your men better throw down your guns,' he called. 'You're finished around here.'

156

A gun blasted instantly from the shadows, and Kelf fired at the muzzle flash. He stayed close to the wall of the store and triggered his gun until the hammer struck an empty chamber. He was able to aim his last three shots because the muzzle flame of several guns cast a dim illumination between him and Stratton's men and, as he reloaded the chambers of his gun with fresh cartridges from his belt, he could hear shouts and cries of pain mingled with the sound of hoofs rattling on the sun-baked ground.

Slugs were blasting the mouth of the alley where he stood and he dropped to one knee, bringing his gun into action once more. He could hear shooting in other parts of the town, and guessed that Carter's posse men were buying into the shoot-out. His accurate shooting had overwhelmed the men facing him and only stray shots came his way. He returned shot for shot, and the gun flashes ahead of him faded away until he was able to stand and await developments.

Shooting sounded in Main Street and he hurried along the alley to where it joined the street. At least six men were attacking the law office, and fierce shooting was coming from the building. He closed in, staying in the shadows, and when he heard Abel Stratton's voice encouraging his men from the far side of the jail, he eased forward until he could see figures in a rough half circle in the street, pouring shots at the beleaguered lawmen.

When he began to shoot at the attackers, they

dropped out of the fight, and then they were running away along the street; Kelf's deadly accurate fire had tipped the balance. He went close to the front door of the jail and called, identifying himself. Carter's voice replied, and the next instant the sheriff emerged from the office and paused at Kelf's side.

'We chased them out from the back of the jail,' Carter said in a highly satisfied tone. 'I think we've got them now. I reckoned they'd run into the big saloon to make a last stand, and my posse will be moving in to surround the place. Come on, let's get into the action before it's over.'

Kelf went with the sheriff along the boardwalk towards the saloon. Desultory shooting was taking place in different parts of the town. But Kelf was interested only in Stratton, aware that nothing would be settled until the rancher was down and finished. Several men came out of the saloon at a run and kept moving. Three men arrived at the batwings as Kelf and Carter got there.

Carter led the way into the saloon, gun in hand, and Kelf followed, thumbing fresh shells into his gun. Kelf's keen gaze took in the scene of Abel Stratton confronting a tall man who was standing behind the bar. Six range-clad men were huddled around Stratton, pistols out, eyes searching for the first signs of resistance in the man.

'Serve drinks, Redfern,' Stratton said. His face was a mask of evil intent, and he waved a pistol under

Redfern's nose.

'You've had your last free drink in here, Stratton. You're finished now. The law has taken over.'

'I own this town and everyone in it. The ground the town is built on is my range. I own everything. You don't own a damn thing.' Stratton jerked a burning lamp off a small shelf and threw it down behind the bar. Flames sprang up.

Redfern leapt back, splashed by kerosene, his pants legs beginning to flame. He reached under the counter and his hands came up filled with a shot gun. Stratton jerked his pistol into the aim and sent a shot into the barman's chest. Redfern went over backwards, his weapon exploding harmlessly, the load of buckshot raking the ceiling. The men around Stratton started shooting indiscriminately. Carter began shooting, and his posse men in the big room added their hot lead to the fray.

Kelf watched Stratton. The rancher ducked behind his men and ran for the back door. Kelf lifted his pistol and fired as Stratton pushed open the door. Stratton staggered, leaned against the doorway, and turned towards Kelf, glaring at him as he raised his gun and took aim. Kelf fired from the hip and Abel Stratton fell over backwards as if his feet had been kicked from under him. Kelf lifted his gun, and at that moment, a slug hit him at close quarters. He felt as if he had been struck by lightning, and knew nothing more, heard none of the gun thunder as the posse men killed or arrested Stratton's men. As the shooting faded, Carter found Kelf lying on his back with blood dribbling from a bullet hole neatly drilled high in his chest. . . .

Tower Rock was silent when Kelf opened his eyes in the early hours of the next morning. He was in a hotel room, and was surprised to see Adelaide Stratton sitting beside his bed in attendance. She came to his side when he moved and groaned, and placed a cool hand on his brow.

'What happened?' he asked.

'Be quiet and rest,' she replied. 'The doctor said you must take it easy. You'll be on your back for at least two weeks. Go to sleep now.'

'If you don't tell me what happened I shan't be able to sleep,' he protested.

'There isn't much to tell.' Her voice was unemotional. 'My father was killed in that last shoot-out and those of his crew that survived have been arrested. Willard was shot accidently by one of his own men in the attack on the jail and died instantly. That's all there is to tell. I'm the new owner of the Stratton place and I'm not looking forward to the prospect. Will you help me when you're back on your feet?'

Kelf reached out a hand and she clasped it as if it were a lifeline. He nodded and groaned, and then lost consciousness again, but he was smiling faintly. . . .